DEATH AT THE YELLOW ROSE

After another punishing winter spent herding steers up the Chisholm Trail, ageing cowboy Chris Bridges takes a job in the Yellow Rose saloon, figuring life will be easier from now on. He could not be more wrong. Framed for the murder of a young girl, his attempts to clear his name see him linking up with a New York detective investigating a mysterious racket. Bridges is learning that life in town can be every bit as hazardous as that on the trail . . .

BRENT LARSSEN

DEATH AT THE YELLOW ROSE

Complete and Unabridged

LINFORD
Leicester

First published in Great Britain in 2014 by
Robert Hale Limited
London

First Linford Edition
published 2016
by arrangement with
Robert Hale Limited
London

A catalogue record for this book is available
from the British Library.

ISBN 978–1–4448–2717–0

Published by
F. A. Thorpe (Publishing)
Anstey, Leicestershire

Set by Words & Graphics Ltd.
Anstey, Leicestershire
Printed and bound in Great Britain by
T. J. International Ltd., Padstow, Cornwall

This book is printed on acid-free paper

1

Chris Bridges was beginning to feel old. It was not just that, at forty-two years of age, his waist was thicker and his breath shorter than had been the case even a year or two earlier. When he shaved that morning he had noticed for the first time that many of the bristles on his chin were now white. Long, wispy hairs were also sprouting from the tips of his ears, giving him a lynx-like appearance and, as if all that were not enough, he had overheard one of the younger men refer to him as 'that old-timer'. It was all very sobering and disagreeable.

Even without these reflections, Bridges knew that he simply could not face the trail again that year. It was early October now and it had taken them six weeks to work their way up the Chisholm Trail from Texas, herding 2,500 longhorn steers to the railhead here in Stockton. He purely could not face sleeping out at night again for now, nor even working outdoors for a spell if the truth were to be told. He needed to stay in the warm like other folk in the town at this time of year, only venturing out into the cold when he had a powerful good reason for doing so.

If he were going to stay in Stockton for the winter, then Bridges figured that he would need some sort of work and also a place to stay. Problem was that he didn't have all that many skills such as would make him attractive to some potential employer. He could ride as good as he could walk, use his fists and shoot straight; but there was no shortage at all of men like that in any cattle town. They were a drag on the market.

Now truth is sometimes stranger than fiction, and this proved to be the case when Chris Bridges went to the Yellow Rose saloon that afternoon to think things over. The first thing the barkeep, who knew him a little, said when he fetched up there was,

'Hey, you know anybody looking for a job?'

'What kind of a job?' asked Bridges curiously.

'Helping out here. Nothing too strenuous, if you discount throwing out the occasional drunk. Other than that, just picking up glasses, serving customers and generally helping out.'

'Well, I might be interested myself,' said Bridges.

'You?' said the man dubiously. 'Thought you was just a cowboy. You ever work in a bar before?'

'Well, I been in enough saloons,' Bridges said. 'I pretty much know what's what.'

The barkeep, whose name was Kirby, eyed Bridges up appraisingly. 'Well,' he said, 'I reckon you look like a fellow who can take care of himself and that is the main qualification needed to work here. I tell you now, the money is not so great, but you get a room upstairs and you can eat here as well.'

And so it was that when the rest of the crew headed back to Texas, Chris Bridges stayed on in Stockton, living and working at the Yellow Rose.

It only took a day or two of working at the saloon for Bridges to realize that the man who had hired him had not been altogether straight about what was entailed. 'Throwing out the occasional drunk' meant in reality dealing with a constant stream of rough customers who would like as not take a swing at him as well as anybody else. Keeping order in the Yellow Rose by spotting and throwing out the troublemakers was really the chief of his duties, with collecting empty glasses and suchlike being only a minor and insignificant part of the work. It was something that Bridges had never really noticed when he had been a customer himself at the place, but now that he was working there, it seemed to him that he was having to wrastle with some fighting-drunk madman every few minutes of his working day.

'How is it, Kirby,' asked Bridges, after an especially lively encounter with a pair of rowdy cowboys had left him with a split lip, 'How is it that you did not at first tell me when I took this job that much of the work would involve rough-housing in this way?'

'Oh, I never emphasize that aspect of the thing when hiring staff,' said Kirby, with disarming candour. 'On account of it might discourage folk from working here. Those that take the job are most of 'em fellows like you with nowhere else to go and so they tend to stay on in spite of all the fighting.'

Bridges shook his head in disgust. 'You are something else again, Kirby, you know that?'

The man smiled brightly. 'Why, thank you!'

'No,' said Bridges. 'It was not meant to be in the nature of a compliment.'

Strange as it may seem, until he landed that job in the Yellow Rose, Chris Bridges had never before lived in a town. Sure, he had spent a few days here and there in various cattle towns at the end of the trail, but he had only ever lived on farms and ranches. He had been born on a farm and the closest thing he had had to a home in recent years was a bunkhouse in Texas. Most of the fellows who lived so were in their twenties or younger and he sometimes tried to figure out how it was that at forty-two years of age he was still stuck in that way of life.

The little room which Bridges had, right at the top of the building, was comfortable enough. He acquired a little stove which ran on lamp oil and this warmed the place up at night. The Yellow Rose was the biggest of the eight saloons in Stockton and it had two floors of rooms above the bar-room. The first floor was, Bridges supposed, something like a hotel. At any rate, rooms were rented out there. It was while he was passing up to his own room on the top floor one night that he first encountered Marion, an attractive young redhead, perhaps eighteen or nineteen years of age. The two of them literally bumped into each other on the staircase.

'I do beg your pardon, ma'am,' said Bridges, when he nearly knocked the slim young girl over as he hurried up the dimly lit stairs. 'I hope I have not hurt you?'

'Lord,' said the girl, 'it would take a sight more than that to hurt *me*. I do not recollect seeing you here before. Are you Kirby's new man?'

'In a manner of speaking,' said Bridges, 'I suppose that I am. Are you staying here too, ma'am?'

The girl giggled. 'Less of the 'ma'am'. There is no occasion to be formal with me. No, I am not staying here. I visit from time to time, though.'

'Well, I hope that we shall meet again.'

'If you're living up by the roof, then I make no doubt we will. There being only this one staircase, I mean. We are sure to be bumping into each other pretty regular. Not so violently as just now though, or so I hope.'

Bridges began to stammer another apology, but the girl cut him short. 'It is nothing to speak of. I am only having some fun with you.'

'Well, goodnight ma ... I don't rightly know what I should call you?'

'My name is Marion. That will do well enough.'

'My name is Bridges, that is to say Chris. Chris Bridges. Goodnight, Marion.'

'Goodnight, Chris.'

After Bridges had carried on up to his room, the girl stood smiling to herself for a second or so. There was something old fashioned and almost gentlemanly about the man, despite his rough voice and uncultivated manners.

★ ★ ★

The night after Bridges first met Marion there occurred one of those incidents that could only have chanced in a place associated with William

Kirby. It happened in this wise.

Although cow towns like Abilene, Dodge and the rest had reputations for violence and gunplay, in reality very few people died of gunshot wounds. The murder rate in Abilene, for instance, was only fifteen in ten years. There were parts of New York City which saw more violent deaths than that in a decade. Still and all, men *did* die from bullet wounds from time to time. As long as such deaths were a result of fair fights and not ambushes from behind, the law did not take too strong a view of them.

Kirby, who both owned and ran the Yellow Rose, was a man who was crooked by nature. He would always sooner lie or steal than handle matters in a straightforward fashion. So averse was he to plain dealing that even when honesty would serve him better, he still resorted to trickery and deceit.

On this particular night Kirby finally managed to clear the bar at around two in the morning. He and Bridges between them succeeded in getting all the drinkers out, even two men who had drunk themselves into a stupor and were asleep beneath the tables. Bridges then began wiping the tables and putting the chairs on them, ready for the floor being swept in the morning. It was while doing this that he came across a fellow sitting alone in the shadows, the one man that he and Kirby had seemingly missed.

'Hey, fella,' said Bridges, shaking the man's shoulder roughly. 'Hey, wake up.' He gripped a little harder and shook the fellow more briskly, whereupon the man fell to the floor. What was odd was that he did not change his position and lay on the floor in the same pose as he had been sitting in the chair; as though he had been a shop-window dummy.

'That's blazing strange!' muttered Bridges to himself. He bent down and touched the man's face, before jerking his hand back in revulsion. The skin he touched was as cold as a piece of fish.

'Hey, Kirby,' Bridges called. 'There's something wrong here.' The barkeep came over irritably.

'What's the case?' asked Kirby. Seeing the figure on the floor, he said, 'Just throw him out into the street, Bridges.'

'He ain't drunk,' said Bridges. 'Truth is, I think he's dead.'

'Ah, shit! That's all I need. Are you sure?'

'You want I should run fetch the doctor?'

'No, you damned fool. And have a lot of questions? Let me have a look at him.' Kirby squatted down beside the prostrate figure and began slapping his face and twisting his arm. The man's arm was not loose and flexible, like it would be with a man who was asleep or unconscious. It was so stiff and unyielding that when Kirby twisted it, the rest of the body moved with it.

'Strikes me,' said Bridges, 'as though that fellow has been dead for some hours. That there is what they call the rigor. It sets in some time after death.'

'What the hell's wrong with you,

Bridges? You think that you are giving evidence in a coroner's court or some such? I don't give a damn how long he's been dead. The point is, what are we going to do about him?'

'Well, I guess I could go and report the death to the sheriff,' said Bridges uncertainly, quite unable to see what Kirby was driving at.

'No, that won't answer. It's Thursday. We got Friday and Saturday coming up. They're our busy nights. If there is some unexplained death then we will have the place closed down and I don't know what all else trouble.'

Still Bridges did not grasp the way that Kirby's thoughts were tending. He said, 'Well, I reckon we have to tell somebody what has happened here. We can't just throw a corpse out into the street like we would a drunk.'

'No,' said Kirby, wistfully. 'That would still invite questions. I have seen cases such as this before and it is the very devil. Before you know it, somebody will be saying that he was

12

poisoned by something he drank here, or that he was murdered or some such. Either way, it would be bad for business. No, I must make it look like a straightforward case of homicide in self-defence. I cannot afford to have this place closed down while a lot of damn-fool questions are asked.'

'Kirby,' said Bridges in perplexity, 'I do not understand this conversation at all. Who was defending themself against a dead man? It makes no sense.'

Kirby gave a sidelong glance, which was full of cunning. 'What I propose in plain language is this. I shall fire a shot from yon fellow's gun and also one from my own into his heart. I shall then say that he attacked me and that I killed him while defending myself against his murderous attack. You will back me up in this, I dare say?'

'You will disfigure this dead man in order to save yourself the trouble of having this place closed down for a few days?' asked Bridges in amazement. 'It is not to be thought of; I will have no

13

part in the matter.'

'Well then,' said Kirby, seeing that Bridges was not about to be persuaded into condoning his plan, 'just go upstairs and do not set mind if you hear a couple of shots. Only keep quiet about this, that is all I ask and I shall give you some extra money this week.'

'I will remain silent, but I do not want your blood money. I never heard of anything like it in my life. You will go too far one day, Kirby and that is a fact.'

A few minutes after climbing into his bed, Bridges heard two pistol shots from the bar and assumed that Kirby had put into execution his plan.

To Bridges's astonishment, everything worked out just as Kirby had planned. Nobody came along to claim the dead man as a friend. The fact that he had died and nobody had noticed suggested that he had been drinking alone in the saloon and the general view was that he had been some saddle tramp who had just got liquored-up and decided to shoot somebody. Kirby came out of the matter without a stain on his character and did not have to close the place down on Friday and Saturday as he would have, had there been an unexplained death.

* * *

Over the next week or so Bridges encountered the girl called Marion a couple of times and plucked up the courage from somewhere to ask her if she would care to visit the newly opened musical theatre with him one night. The surprised look which she gave him when he suggested this made him think that he had got above himself and perhaps offended the young woman.

Howsoever, she said at length, 'Yes, sure I'll go there with you. I have had a hankering after doing so, but have not yet had an opportunity. You do not mind being seen with me out and about?'

15

'Mind?' said Bridges, 'Why should I mind? It is you who might mind to be seen in the company of a man such as me.'

The girl shook her head wonderingly. 'You are a strange one and no mistake, Chris Bridges. When should you like to go to this entertainment?'

'I have the Wednesday evening off,' Bridges said.

'Wednesday it is,' said Marion, still looking at him in that queer way that he could not quite fathom.

2

Bridges had invited Marion on the Saturday to visit the musical theatre with him. The following day being Sunday, he decided, for a novelty, to attend church. He set out upon this enterprise not through any religious conviction, but rather in the spirit of one who is determined to sample all that town life has to offer, whether it be a new kind of saloon or divine worship.

To his surprise, Bridges found the service pretty moving. The preacher talked of the brotherhood of man and how we should not distinguish between men according to their race or creed; only seeing them all as fellow men and brothers. Since this was how he himself saw the case, never having bothered his head about the colour of a man's skin and similar such things, Bridges felt that this fellow was on the right track.

He had not been to church since he was a boy and, after hearing such sensible views being expounded, he thought that he might find his way there again the following Sunday. That was until he chanced upon the preacher in his private capacity the next day.

When he entered the general store on Monday morning, Bridges recognized at once the smooth voice of the preacher who, the previous day, had had so much to say about the brotherhood of man. A small group of customers was gathered around him as he spoke feelingly of what he saw as one of the town's chief problems.

'And then there's not only those Mexicans. There's a nest of half-breeds too. Such men combine all the savageness and ferocity of the redskin with the worst features of the white man. Every day, these types become more impudent and why it is put up with is a complete mystery to me.'

The preacher caught sight of Bridges and said, 'Wouldn't you say so, sir? This town needs a little cleaning up is what I am contending.'

Bridges stared at the man for a moment, before saying contemptuously, 'You was singing a different song in your pulpit yesterday, Reverend.' He turned on his heel and left the store.

This one small incident just about summed up how Bridges's thoughts had lately been tending as regards living in a town. On the trail, men said what they thought and then stuck to it. If you didn't care for a fellow, then you steered clear of him. Here in town, the people always seemed to be saying one thing and then next time you came across them, they were speaking differently. They would be sweet to your face and then as soon as your back was turned on them, they began to deride you. This was not at all how Bridges liked to live.

Hearing the preacher from the church behaving in this two-faced way was a shock. One day, he's going on about loving his fellow man and the next talking about the impudence of 'half-breeds'. To Bridges, this kind of thing was just plain disgusting. Maybe, he thought, this is the consequence of living in towns, with all the folk huddled together in this way. It does not strike me as a healthy arrangement.

The musical theatre to which Chris Bridges had invited young Marion was a new draw in town. The place had been converted from a closed-down saloon and it was similar in many ways to the other saloons in town. The chief difference was that along one side of the bar-room was a stage and on this various acts took place: dancing, singing, juggling, tumblers and a whole heap of other things.

'I declare,' said Marion, with a childlike pleasure, 'this is as good as a play!' She looked around her with shining eyes, obviously enchanted at the place.

To Bridges, the whole thing had a slightly tawdry air about it, but he was pleased to find that his companion was enjoying herself. They secured a table near the stage and settled down to watch the acts. It was plain to Bridges that the money here was being made on the food and drinks, both of which were outrageously overpriced. Still and all, it was worth it to see the young girl's simple pleasure at the entertainment being offered.

One thing he did mark was that Marion seemed to be very well known and popular.

'How is it,' Bridges enquired, after the sixth or seventh man had hailed her, 'how is it that everybody appears to know you?'

'Oh, you know how it is. I get around. Hush now, I want to hear the singing.'

At the interval between acts, Bridges said to Marion, 'I do not recollect that you ever told me where you live and work?'

The girl laughed. 'That's no great secret. I work up at the hurdy. I have a room near by.'

'The hurdy?' asked Bridges, 'I am not sure that I understand you.'

'The hurdy-gurdy house,' she said impatiently, 'You must know it, it is called the Golden Eagle.'

'You are a saloon girl?' he asked in surprise.

Marion gave him a sharp look. 'Yes, what of it?'

'Nothing. Nothing at all. I was just a little surprised is all.'

'A girl's got to make her way as best she can. There are worse ways of doing so than dancing in a hurdy.'

'Yes,' said Bridges, a little embarrassed. 'Yes, I am sure that this is so. Forgive me, I know little about it.'

During the next turn, which was two clowns who were also quite skilful acrobats, Bridges thought the matter over. He himself had always preferred the old-fashioned type of saloon like the Yellow Rose; the kind of place where you just did not see any women at all. He knew that some of those with whom he had ridden favoured instead dance halls and other, even less salubrious establishments. Bridges's view of the case was simple: saloons were for men and nice girls stayed well away from them.

He had noticed that there were a few women in this house, seated at tables seemingly by themselves and watching the show. There was something faintly shocking about this, although he could not rightly have said why.

The presence of women in the musical theatre seemed to have a moderating effect upon the behaviour of the men who were present. Scuffles, brawls and even the occasional knife fight were not uncommon at the Yellow Rose, but there was nothing of the sort here.

When trouble did erupt, it was Bridges himself who provoked it. He had been getting a little irritated by the way in which various men waved at Marion and greeted her with what he felt was a lack of proper respect or common courtesy. One fellow came up to their table and said to his companion,

'Hell Marion, I didn't recognize you, with you so covered up and all!' It was enough for Bridges. He stood up and said to the man:

'You had best apologize to the lady for that remark, friend, else you and me are going to fall out.'

The man looked a mite taken aback, but eventually laughed and said to Marion, 'I am sorry if you was offended by my remark. There was, as you might know, nothing meant by it.' He then nodded amiably enough at Bridges and went on his way.

'What did you do that for?' asked Marion. 'You will queer my pitch if you do not set mind to what you are about. I will thank you not to start trouble which centres around me. I am well able to take care of my own self.'

Before Bridges had had a chance to respond to this, a tough-looking man of about the same age as him sidled by Marion and, as he squeezed past, ran a hand over her shoulder. This was not to be endured and Bridges was on his feet again in an instant.

'What do you mean by it?' he asked the man. 'Would you wish for somebody to treat your own wife or daughter in that way?'

The man gave a short laugh, which sounded more like the bark of a dog with an uncertain temper.

'Ain't got neither a wife nor daughters, as far as that goes,' he said in what sounded like a Southern accent. 'Anyways, what affair is it of yours?'

'I will show you just exactly what affair it is of mine, if you will favour me with your company outside for some minutes.'

'You say what?' responded the man in amazement. 'You will fight me for her honour?'

'Yes,' said Bridges quietly. 'That is the way of it.'

'This is the damnedest thing I ever heard tell of,' said the man, who was obviously stumped to know how to handle the situation. 'You will fight me over the favours of some two-bit saloon girl?'

The words were scarcely out of his mouth, when Bridges had him by the shirt front and began dragging him out of the bar-room. He managed to get a tighter hold on the fellow by twisting his arm up behind his back and he did not set mind to how many drinks were knocked off people's tables as he pulled and pushed the man outside. They were both of them wearing pistols, but the thing had happened too fast for anybody to even consider drawing.

'You have just made the biggest mistake of your natural life!' said the man whom Bridges had ejected with so little ceremony from the musical theatre.

'Well,' said Bridges, 'what will you have? Are you going to ask pardon for the liberty you took with the lady?'

Rather than ask pardon, the man chose to reach for his gun. Whether he had Bridges pegged for some slow-witted country bumpkin or whether there was another cause, the fact is that he did not pull his pistol in a great hurry. He just reached his hand down in a casual way as though looking for something in his pocket. Perhaps that very casualness was part of his act and deceived others into thinking that he was not about to draw on them. Whether or no, Bridges saw the play and his own gun was out and cocked ready before the other man's pistol was clear of the holster. Hearing the sharp metallic click as Bridges cocked his piece, the fellow's arm froze and he made no attempt to see if he could shoot Bridges before the other had time to squeeze the trigger.

The two of them stood in the road like this for a few seconds, frozen like shop-window manikins. Then the man let his gun fall back into the holster and very slowly moved his hand clear.

'You got the pull on me there right enough,' he said, 'What is your aim now? To kill an unarmed man?'

Bridges felt somehow wrong-footed by all this and limited himself to observing, 'I hope that we do not meet again in a hurry.' He then backed into the theatre, never once taking his eyes off the other man.

If Marion had been annoyed at Bridges for the way he spoke to the first man whom he felt had insulted her, it was nothing to the way that she raged at him when he returned to the table after his confrontation in the street. She was that angry, she could hardly get out the words.

'What the hell do you think you are doing? I do not want that particular man for my enemy, even if you do.'

'I do not want anybody for my enemy,' observed Bridges mildly. 'But nor will I sit here and see a lady under my protection being insulted or mauled about in that wise.'

'I am leaving. The evening is over.' Saying which, the girl stood up and walked out without further ado, leaving

Bridges sitting there and feeling uncommonly foolish.

★ ★ ★

There being nothing more to do, Bridges made his way back to the Yellow Rose. He had forgotten that it was a big evening. A week ago two men had engaged in a wager while drinking there as to whether it was possible to play a whole, entire game of billiards with both parties mounted on horse-back. Kirby had agreed that the bet could be settled at his billiard table.

Now it might seem strange that the owner of a saloon would agree to having his bar messed up by men riding their horses into it, but it was really in the interests of the saloons to go along with foolishness of this sort. Towns like Stockton, Abilene and the rest owed their prosperity to the cowboys who spent their cash there as soon as they got paid off at the end of the trail.

One way or the other, either in the

saloons or brothels, those boys generally disposed of the whole of their wages in those cow towns before they headed back south. It could be a nuisance, putting up with a set of drunken cowboys making whoopee, but it was a tolerably profitable nuisance for those running the cathouses, stores and saloons.

Touching upon the bet about the horseback game of billiards, Kirby knew that there was a lot of money riding on the outcome. Many of the men who frequented the saloons would bet upon quite literally anything at all. Of course poker and faro were played for high stakes, but that was not the whole story, not by a long sight. If there was no regular card game running, some of the boys might wager twenty dollars on whether it would rain before midday or if the next person to enter the store would be male or female.

By allowing the horseback game of billiards, Kirby might have been running the risk of having to clean a pile of horseshit from his floor, but he would make so much in the drinks bought by those with money riding on the outcome of the wager that that was pretty small beer in comparison.

Bridges was astonished at the number of customers crowded into the Yellow Rose. He had guessed that it would be a busy night, which was why he was glad not to be working that evening, but he could not have guessed that there would be quite this many men. Almost the first person he saw when he walked through the door was the fellow with whom he had had the showdown earlier. He was talking to Kirby in an animated fashion, and now he thought about it, Bridges seemed to recall having seen the man there before. Which probably meant the fellow had come here to complain about him to Kirby, perhaps with a view to having him lose his job.

It did not look to Bridges as though any useful purpose would be served by talking the matter over right then with either Kirby or the man he had drawn on. There was too much liquor flowing for that to lead to any sort of peaceful resolution at this time of night, not to mention that he did not want to get roped into helping out on such a busy occasion as this on his night off. That being so, he decided to go for a quiet walk before turning in for the night.

It seemed to be Chris Bridges's night for getting into scrapes, because he had got only a few yards along the road before coming across something he didn't much like the look of. Two men were guiding a young girl along the sidewalk, one on either side. To Bridges's eye, this child could have been no more than fourteen or fifteen years old and she looked to him as though she had been drinking. Her step was unsteady and she was leaning heavily on one of the men.

He also observed that both men appeared to be gripping her arms in a way which suggested less that they were supporting her and more that she was being prevented from leaving them of her own free will. It would have sat ill with Bridges to turn a blind eye to such a business and so he walked up to the group and said,

'Pardon me for intruding, but I am thinking that something is not right here. Who is that girl and where are you taking her?'

'What's it got to do with you, you cow's son?' said one of the men in a low, ugly voice. 'You best make tracks; you hear what I'm telling you?'

'That is not the best way of persuading me that there is nothing wrong here,' said Bridges. 'I will ask again, who is that child and what is going on that you look to be taking her somewhere against her wishes?'

The second man responded in what he clearly thought was a reassuring way.

'It's nothing to be alarmed at, my friend. This here is my young cousin and she has fell in with the wrong crowd. She has been drinking hard liquor and I don't know what all else.

Still, it is heartwarming to find a stranger like yourself who shows such concern. We are now taking her home to her folks and so we will be bidding you goodnight.'

None of this rang true and Bridges was still weighing up what he was going to do about it, when the girl herself broke in, crying,

'Oh help me! They are taking me the Lord knows where and I don't want to go with them. I am not drunk, they put something over my mouth which made me fall asleep.'

It was very obvious that there was some villainy afoot and so, for the second time that night, Bridges drew his pistol, saying to the two men,

'You best unhand that child. Do not get crosswise to me or you will be sorry.'

The men looked at each other, at a loss to know how to handle this development.

Bridges reached out and took the girl's arm, saying to her, 'Don't be afeared, I will protect you.'

To the two men, he said softly, 'Let go of her there.' To his vast surprise, they did so.

So far, all this had happened without drawing the least attention from any of those passing by in the dark street and it struck Bridges that the men were keen to keep things that way. Whatever it was that they were about, they did not want ordinary, decent people to know about it.

The first man who had spoken to him said, 'You do not know what you are mixing yourself up in, fellow. If I was you, I would just back away now and leave this alone. The girl is nothing to you; why should you hazard yourself in this way?'

'She is little more than a child by the look of her,' said Bridges. 'It is everybody's business to see that such as she are protected.'

The second man said, 'We will not engage in a gunfight here in the street, but be assured that there will be a reckoning if you meddle in this. My advice to you would be to let it be.'

'Nothing of the sort,' said Bridges. 'I shall take this child with me and look into this matter. I tell you straight, if you want trouble, then I will provide all that you require. This girl is not going off with you two.'

Having said which, he began retreating back towards the Yellow Rose, watching the men the whole time. They watched him too, and it was inevitable that they should see when he entered the saloon.

The girl was still shaky and none too steady on her feet, but she appeared to understand that Bridges was looking after her. She clung trustingly to his arm. It went against the grain for him to lead any female, let alone one of such tender years, into a saloon but, as he saw it, he had no other choice. He helped the child up the stairs and took her to his room at the top of the building. Once there, he allowed her to lie on the bed, while he lit the lamp and tried to figure out what to do next.

It says something about a man like Chris Bridges that at no stage in these proceedings did it occur to him that he might be putting himself into a false position by having a young girl up in his room in this way. His single aim was to look after her and restore her to her family.

After she had rested for a few minutes, he asked her, 'Tell me now, what is your name?'

'I am Ellie. Ellie Cartwright. Thank you for taking care of me back there.'

'That doesn't signify,' said Bridges. 'How old are you, Ellie?'

'I am sixteen.'

'Sixteen?' he said. 'I thought you was younger than that. Who are those men?'

'My step-pa owes them a deal of money. They told him that he could clear the debt if I did some little work for them.'

'What did your ma say of this?'

'She is scared of him. She went along with it 'cause she was in fear.'

'So what happened? They came to collect you or what?'

'Yes, they turned up with a buggy and when once I was in it they told me that I had to be a good girl and do as they bid me.'

'What might that have been?'

'They told me that I must not be over-modest and that I would be expected to take off . . . take off my clothes.' At this, the child began sobbing and Bridges thought that he had found out enough for now. He sat quietly and let the girl cry herself out a little. When she was a little calmer, he said:

'Did they drug you or aught?'

'Yes,' she replied. 'I started screaming and one of them held something over my mouth and I passed out. When I came to, I was as you saw me, walking along the street with them.'

'Where do you live?'

The girl gave him her address and Bridges tried to reckon out the right course of action to deal with what was to him a very unusual state of affairs. He supposed that a visit to the sheriff's office would be the first thing to do.

The difficulty as he saw it was that he could not leave the girl here, because he was certain-sure that the men who had took her had marked where he had come with her. Not to mention that he was not even sure that the sheriff would be in his office at that time of night.

The more he mulled the thing over, the more it seemed to him that the best dodge would be for him to let the girl sleep in his bed this night, while he sat watch over her. In the morning, they could both make their way to the sheriff in broad daylight and she could tell her story there.

A natural delicacy caused Bridges to be a little hesitant in outlining this scheme to the frightened girl, but as soon as he had done so she expressed her gratitude and showed complete trust in him. He was not used to another human being depending upon him so entirely and if it was a novel experience, it was also a pleasing one. He laid the blanket around her and then sat down on the chair to wait out the night.

The hours crawled by slowly. There are few duller things than just sitting in a chair and waiting for time to pass. Every so often, Bridges would get up and take a turn about the room to stretch his legs. He had no watch and so could only gauge the hour by the noises he heard in the street. When things had quietened down a little, he figured it must be around 2 a.m. Some little time after this, he heard a soft and hesitant knocking on the door.

'Who is it?' he enquired softly, not wanting to wake the sleeping girl. There was a mumbled response, which could have been from either a man or a woman. He went to the door and unbolted it. Then he cautiously opened it a crack, whereupon somebody on the other side kicked the door with his full force, sending Bridges flying back into the room. He was already dazed when two figures rushed into the room, one of whom swiped him round the head with a lead-weighted blackjack. He lost consciousness immediately.

3

When Bridges came to it took him some little time to recollect where he was and what was going on. It was seemingly just after dawn, and to his confusion he was not alone in the tiny room. Three men were crowded around him, one of whom was slapping him around the face to rouse him to consciousness.

'Hey, wake up there, you dog!' said the man hitting him. Bridges put up his hand and grabbed the fellow's wrist, whereupon another man gave him a jab in the ribs from behind.

Now Bridges was not a man to allow others to take liberties in this way and he could handle himself in a fight as well as anybody. He was just on the point of jumping up and setting to, when the third man, who was standing by the bed, turned round.

It was the sheriff. Bridges knew him by sight, but had never had cause to speak to him. The fact that these men who were roughing him about were the law came as a sobering and disagreeable shock. It was then that he saw what lay on the bed.

Ellie looked at first as though she were sleeping peacefully. It was not until you saw the livid red marks on her throat and noticed that she was not actually breathing, that you might suspect that all was not as it should be. Bridges sat up and stared at the girl in horror.

'Yes, you whoreson, you look upon your work!' said the sheriff, gazing at Bridges as though he were the lowest form of creeping life imaginable.

'What's going on?' said Bridges, stunned at the realization that his efforts to protect the child had been all in vain.

'Yes, well may you ask that question,' said the sheriff. 'It all looks plain enough from where I am stood. You somehow persuaded this poor child up into your room and then you strangled her. What happened? Did she resist your advances?'

'This is not at all as it appears,' said Bridges. 'There has been some species of misunderstanding here.'

'I'll be bound,' said the man who had been slapping his face to rouse him. 'The misunderstanding being that you thought you could commit murder and then get away with it. That is certainly by way of being a misunderstanding on your part.'

Bridges shook his head. 'No, I mean as to the fate of that poor girl. I rescued her and brought her up here to keep her safe from harm. I purposed to bring her to the sheriff's office this very morning, for her to be restored to her family.'

It was tolerably plain to Bridges that none of the three men in that room along with him gave any sort of credence to this claim. He was hauled to his feet and his wrists were handcuffed behind his back. Then he was led downstairs and out into the street.

Word had somehow got around, because despite the early hour, there was a group of men outside the Yellow Rose, men who began calling out insults and threats as soon as they caught sight of him in the custody of the sheriff and his men. Somebody must have tipped them the wink, because they were fully aware that a young girl had been killed. Among the shouts of anger were menacing calls for him to be strung up there and then.

The jail at the back of the sheriff's office was little bigger than a broom-closet. It consisted simply of an alcove with stout steel bars fixed from ceiling to wall to keep the prisoner penned in. There was just about room for the single bunk and the only sanitation was a beat up, galvanized steel pail in the corner. The place smelt like a privy.

It was here that Bridges was locked up, pending enquiries, although as the sheriff pointed out, there was little need for such formalities, the case being an open and shut one.

Lying on the bunk, Bridges tried to reason the case out. It didn't take much thinking to work out that the girl had been killed by those who had been in charge of her when first he encountered her. That much was clear. But why had she been killed, once he was knocked out? Why didn't they just take her away and carry on with whatever beastliness they had planned?

Try as he might, Bridges could not seem to see any reason in it. Those fellows could not have had too much of a grudge against him for drawing down on them in the street, at least not such a serious one that they would commit murder to satisfy it. It was a regular conundrum, of which he was wholly unable to make any sort of sense.

It was while he was racking his brains in this way that the sheriff returned from making his enquiries. Bridges could see at once that these had not worked in his favour.

'I have spoken with two of the people as know you and they both give out the same story,' said the sheriff. 'Which is to say that you are an unnatural sort of man who might be expected to have lusts for children or something else perverted.'

This was so unexpected and ridiculous that Bridges just stared at the sheriff and said nothing at all, waiting to see what would proceed from such a strange beginning.

'I have here a statement from your employer, William Kirby. He says that he thought that you had no interest in grown women and that this worried him. Further states that he saw you on a number of occasions staring in an odd way at little girls.'

Before Bridges could recover from this extraordinary and unlooked-for attack from Kirby, the sheriff continued with,

'I have also spoke to Marion Finch, who by all accounts you were walking out with. She says that you showed no interest in her as a woman and that she had cause to believe that you had an unhealthy interest in children.'

If he had been unable to fathom what the play was before, these latest revelations fairly knocked the wind out of Chris Bridges. That Kirby should tell a heap of lies about him was no great surprise. It was the nature of the lies that was so puzzling. Why should Kirby pretend that he, Bridges, was the sort of fellow to take a shine to little girls?

As for Marion, this was even more baffling. Who had said that he and she had been 'walking out'? He had taken her to that musical theatre the once and had hardly had the opportunity to show any interest in her 'as a woman'!

The sheriff took Bridges's silence for a tacit admission of guilt when faced with new evidence of his depravity.

'I tell you now,' he said, 'I have never met one of you types before. You look normal on the outside, but you must be like some sort of animal deep within. If it was left to me, I would just shoot you like a mad dog.' With which he left Bridges to the consolation of his own thoughts.

After the sheriff was gone Bridges sat up and began to think the matter through again in the light of this new information. Since all this was a pack of lies, whoever was trying to get him hanged must be working together with Marion and Kirby towards that end. There was no chance of misunderstanding or honest mistake in what those two had told the sheriff. It must surely be the case that they had been instructed to lie about him.

As a young man Chris Bridges had had a reputation among some as being a little slow on the uptake. He did not jump swiftly to conclusions and preferred to think things over carefully. His grandma, she would not have it that the boy was slow. She said, 'He ain't slow, he's thorough. Give that boy time and he'll think his way through a brick wall.'

So it proved now, as Bridges ruminated in that little cell. It took him a while, but he eventually came up with the answer.

He was sitting in jail because the girl he had rescued had been killed, probably by those from whose clutches he had freed her. That much was plain. But Marion and Kirby were somehow in on the game as well, going out of their way to help pin a murder on him. Those two knew each other slightly, but not enough, he would have thought, to be in cahoots on something of this nature. The connection must lie elsewhere.

Only a few hours before he had been arrested, he had crossed the man who he thought had been taking a liberty with Marion. That same fellow had turned up at the Yellow Rose. If all this business, being arrested and Kirby and Marion telling lies about him, was of a piece, then that man he had fronted must be the common factor. It followed then that he must also have been involved in that poor child's misfortunes.

Having ciphered all this out most painfully and with a good deal of furrowing of his brow, it came to Bridges that he must get out of there and sort the matter out for his own self. He then spent a further half hour or so, working out the best way to represent the case to the sheriff. When he had done so, he called through the bars of his tiny cell,

'Hey! Hey, you out there. We need to talk.'

The sheriff looked none too keen about the prospect of talking to a man whom he viewed as the killer of a defenceless girl who looked like a child. Still, he came when Bridges hollered and asked him what all the commotion was about.

'I need to get out of here,' Bridges said.

The sheriff guffawed with laughter. 'Yes, you and every other bastard who has ever sat in that there cell. Yes, I'll be bound you do need to get out of there. Was there anything else you might be wanting?'

'Listen,' said Bridges. 'You say that I killed that girl, after she might as it were have rejected my advances. Is that how you figure the case?'

'Yes, I reckon so,' said the sheriff, regarding his prisoner with curiosity. 'What of it?'

'This,' said Bridges. 'The whole thing just don't stack up right. Will you listen to my side of the thing?'

The sheriff was a fair man and although the sight of this fellow made his skin crawl, still and all, he deserved a hearing.

'Let me fetch a chair,' he said, 'and then you can tell me what you claim. Mind, I am not disposed to believe you anything other than a damned libertine who wished to violate that dead girl, but I suppose I should hear what you have to say.'

When the sheriff was settled in the chair which he had brought through from the office, Bridges began to speak.

'First off is that if I was going to molest that girl, do you not think that I would first have taken the precaution of locking and bolting the door? You did not need to bust the door down, did you? Why would I embark upon such a course of action without making sure nobody could walk in on me? It is not sense.'

The sheriff looked hard at Bridges. 'Go on,' he said.

'Then there's this business about me and that Marion walking out together. That's a lot of eyewash, as you would know if you asked around. That night was the first time I ever went anywhere with her and that was only for an hour. 'No interest in her as a woman'? I never heard the like! You have been sold a pup there, we hardly knew each other!'

The sheriff rubbed his chin thoughtfully. 'Keep talking,' was all he said.

'Why, you ain't even asked me yet how I came to be in the room with that girl, nor yet who she was or how she came to be took from her family. Does that not concern this case?'

As Bridges told his story, a terrible doubt crept into Sheriff Tucker's heart, a fear that perhaps he had been a mite hasty about this. It was true that the case had started in a most singular, to say nothing of outright suspicious, way. But when he had entered that room and seen that dead girl, with this man lying near her, seemingly dead drunk, it had all appeared to be so clear-cut and needing no further investigation. Now, listening to Bridges, he was not so sure.

'And another thing,' said Bridges. 'How did you come to hear of this? Who told you to come to that room of mine?'

'Got a letter,' said Tucker, and he sounded like a man who was being defensive about something.

'A letter?' said Bridges in amazement. 'What, you mean through the mail? That's blazing strange to hear!'

'No,' admitted the sheriff, 'it weren't through the mail. Somebody raised

Cain on my front door, around four in the morning. When I went down to see what the case was, there was a note lying there on the mat.'

Bridges was looking at the sheriff like he was viewing a four-legged chicken in a carnival sideshow or something.

'You got a letter from a stranger at four in the morning and didn't consider this odd? I wonder if you are in the right line of work, Sheriff, begging your pardon. What did it say?'

'Said that the help over at the Yellow Rose had been seen taking a young girl to his room and that there had been screaming coming from there, like to suggest that murder had been done.'

'And you and your boys turned up there, found me and thought it was a simple case, with all that was needful was to see me hanged and the matter would be closed? Yes, I see how things stood.'

'I am going to make some more enquiries,' said the sheriff. 'I will go to the farm where you say this girl was taken from and I will also see what your connection with that saloon girl was. Somebody has been telling lies to a peace officer and I am not at all sure that it is not you. We shall see.'

With that, he stood up and took his chair back to the front office. A minute or two later, Bridges heard the door close as Tucker left.

For the rest of the afternoon, Bridges lay on the bunk and tried to relax. He had done all that he could and now he had to see whether or not the sheriff would look into the business properly, or be content with seeing a man hanged whom nobody in town really knew or cared about.

He got his answer at five, when the sheriff returned. He came at once to speak to Bridges.

'I have been out to the Cartwright place and spoke to the mother and stepfather of that girl. I have also had what you might term a long and serious conversation with that girl Marion. On top of which, I talked to your boss.

'First off, what you say about the girl being taken from her home under mysterious circumstances seems to be a true bill. The mother was sporting a black eye and there is something going on there which will bear further investigation. At any rate, the girl left her home last night in the company of men matching the description of those you said you saw her with.

'Mind,' said Sheriff Tucker, as he saw Bridges's face light up with hope, 'That is not to say that you did not have a role in the affair. For aught I know to the contrary, you might have been waiting in that buggy when they fetched her from her home.'

The sheriff went on, 'I also spoke at length to that girl as you took out last night. She admitted that she told me a heap of lies, but will not say who put her to it. I shall look further into that.

'As for your boss, well you might know that he is like a damned corkscrew. I do not place much credence in anything he tells me, especially after that affair of the shooting in self-defence which he worked not so long ago.'

Bridges was growing restless to know where all this was tending. 'So where does this leave me? Are you still aiming to bring me to trial with a view to seeing me hanged?'

The sheriff said nothing for a moment or two, but then produced a key and unlocked the barred gate to the cell.

'I have my doubts about this whole thing,' he said, 'But as things stand, I am not about to lay that murder at your door. I would give you a few words of advice, though.'

'What might those be?' asked Bridges.

'You might have heard of occasions when a peace officer tells a man not to leave town?'

'Yes, I have heard tell of such.'

'My advice to you in the present case is quite the opposite. I advise that you do leave town and that as speedily as you are able. I make no secret of the fact that there is a party or faction in the town which favours lynching you without the formality of a trial. Feelings are running high. Were you to leave town at once, it would make life easier for us all.'

'What?' exclaimed Bridges indignantly. 'You mean I just dig up and leave, with everybody thinking that I have a guilty conscience and could not abide to face the consequences of my actions? No, it is not to be thought of. I will find out what is going on and then clear my name.'

'Do not set your mind to undertaking any sort of vigilante activity. I will not tolerate it for a moment.'

'I am guessing that you have my rifle and pistol from my room here? There is no objection to me having them back?'

'None that I can think of. Only remember what I said about taking the law into your own hands. I tell you, it will not answer.'

As soon as he walked free from that jail cell the only purpose in Chris

Bridges's mind was to find out who had killed the girl whom he had tried to protect from harm. Apart from clearing his own name of the suspicion of such a foul crime, he reckoned that he owed it to the child to bring her murderers to justice. He had pledged himself to take care of her and then by his carelessness had let harm befall her.

He accordingly went to the livery stable where Jake, his gelding, was being looked after, and then rode out to the Cartwright place.

★ ★ ★

Bridges had only the haziest idea of where the farm was to be found, but by riding out in the general direction and stopping to ask various people working in fields, he eventually found the place. It did not look to be a very successful or prosperous enterprise, which went some way towards confirming what the girl had said last night about her step-pa being in debt.

It certainly had the look of a farm where the owner might be struggling to pay his bills. The sun was sinking below the nearby hills as he rode up to the house and dismounted.

There did not at first seem to be anybody at home, when Bridges rapped on the door. After a space though, a rough, surly-looking fellow opened the door and asked Bridges what the hell he was after.

'I am looking to speak to the parents of Ellie, the girl who was killed last night'

'What is it to you? Are you working for the sheriff? We had him up here just a while ago, asking questions. I will not repeat what I said to him.'

'No,' said Bridges, 'it is nothing of that sort. I do not much care what you told the sheriff. Like as not it was a heap of falsehoods. What I am after is something quite different. I want to know who you owed money to and how you came to agree for your stepdaughter to go off in the night like that. Just a name or two will do me fine.'

The man slammed the door, but Bridges was too quick for him, sticking his boot out to prevent the door from closing. From somewhere in the house he heard a woman call, 'Who is it, Jethro?'

'We can talk together,' said Bridges, 'or I can question your wife. Either way, I will not be going from here until I have a plain answer to my questions.'

'She don't know nothing,' said the man. 'Wait here and I will take a turn with you up to yonder field and we can talk there.'

The fellow went off and came back a few minutes later. He and Bridges strolled a distance from the house and then stopped. The sun had gone down and it was nigh on twilight.

'I cannot tell you a lot,' said the man. 'Which is to say that I durst not. I owe money to more than one person. Somebody sold the debt on to a man called 'the colonel'. It was he who told me that I could clear my debt if I let my stepdaughter go off and do some work for them. Before God, that is all I know.'

'This 'colonel', could you favour me with a description of him?'

'Maybe forty, forty-five. Sallow complexion, little mustache, waxed at the ends.'

Bridges was on the point of asking the man where he might be able to lay his hands on this fellow, who he felt sure was the one he had had the disagreement with at the musical theatre the previous night, when there was a sudden and unexpected interruption. The nature of this was the crack of a rifle, fired from a grassy rise some fifty yards away. Bridges was down on the ground with his pistol in his hand almost immediately, but there was only the one shot. Whoever had fired had left the scene without delay.

'Get down, you damned fool!' Bridges said to Cartwright, who replied:

'That's nothing to the purpose. I am killed.'

Bridges glanced up and saw that the other man was holding a hand to his belly. There was a look of bewilderment on his face, rather than pain. He looked puzzled at this turn of events.

Since there had been no more shooting, Bridges stood up and said, 'Can I help you back to the house?'

'No,' said Cartwright, 'I am shot. I feel cold.'

'Here, let me help you to sit down.'

'That does not signify. I will stay on my feet. The bullet is right near my heart. I can feel the pain of it here on my left. I am all but dead.'

'Brace up,' said Bridges. 'While there is life, there is hope. Come, let me assist you.'

The man's legs buckled under him and he fell heavily. The sudden fall must have dislodged the bullet or worked some mischief in Cartwright's vitals, because he snorted loudly, gave a long groan and then lapsed into unconsciousness. A minute later, he stopped breathing.

4

Sheriff Tucker was not best pleased to hear about the death up at the Cartwright farm. He said to Bridges, 'Do you recollect what I said to you, tending towards my views on private vengeance?'

'I didn't shoot him,' said Bridges. 'I'll warrant that if you dig round near to his heart, you will find a minie ball. You are welcome to smell my rifle; it has not been fired for a month. Same goes for my pistol. Here, catch ahold and smell it.' He offered the hilt of the weapon to the sheriff, who waved it away impatiently.

'What I am saying is that you are stirring things up. You had no business going out there to ask questions; this man's death might not have occurred had you kept your distance.'

'I am not at all sure,' said Bridges

slowly, 'that that is so. It was getting dark and the range must have been something more than fifty yards. How if I was the target and they hit the wrong man? You said that feelings were running against me; maybe somebody decided to kill me.'

The sheriff thought this over for a space, before saying, 'It could be so. All the more reason for you not to linger in these parts. Have you nowhere else that you could go?'

'Meaning that you would like to tidy this up by waiting 'til I am a day or so down the trail and then letting it be understood that I killed the girl and her stepfather both? No, I do not think so.'

'Well then, try to stay out of further trouble. Tell me, did Cartwright tell you anything I should know about?'

Bridges did not like telling lies, but neither did he want this man trampling around and muddying up the trail. 'No,' he said, 'Nothing that would help you.'

'If you are staying in Stockton, you will not be able to live at the Yellow Rose,' said the sheriff. 'I dare say that you have thought on this. Do you have anywhere else to go?'

'No, but I have a little money saved. I can go to a boarding house. There are several such in this town.'

'With what is suspected against you, you would be lucky to find one to take you in. If you are determined to stay, then I suppose that I cannot leave you to sleep rough. I know a woman who takes in guests. She lives right on the very edge of town.'

'Will she not also judge me to be a merciless killer and sexual maniac?'

'Not her. She is a God-fearing woman who likes to form her own opinions and not take them ready made from others. It is dark now. If you wish, I will go with you and introduce you to her.'

'Thank you. It is much appreciated.'

★ ★ ★

Mrs Larssen, or the widow Larssen as most people knew her, lived up past the stockyards. Hers was a pretty little house that looked like it would be more at home in New England than this cattle town. It was white-painted clapboard, with a garden running all round it, so that you had to open a little gate before you could even approach the house. Even at that time of year, there was a glorious scented smell from the flowers and vines which were lingering on until the first frost put an end to them.

The sheriff introduced Bridges to the widow Larssen, who was perhaps sixty years of age. Her hair was snow-white and fixed up in a severe and tightly drawn bun. She had the brightest, shrewdest eyes that Bridges had ever seen in a human face, man or woman. There was something birdlike about them, not a friendly and cheery little bird like a sparrow, but rather a raptor: a hawk, maybe. You had the distinct feeling that here was somebody whom it would be hard to put anything across.

Mercifully, this sharp air was blunted a little by the woman's good nature, which also shone through.

'I have heard somewhat of your troubles, Mr Bridges,' she said when once he had been introduced by the sheriff. 'I have a room to rent, that is if you would like to stay here. You will find it a little different from the Yellow Rose, I am afraid.'

Unsure whether this was meant to signify her disapproval of saloons and drinking, Bridges became a little flustered, only for Mrs Larssen to burst into laughter.

'Landsakes, man! I am only joshing with you. You need not think that I am one who is against folks enjoying themselves or having a drink when they are minded to. My shell's not that hard, I hope. Stuart, we need not detain you further, I fancy.' This last was directed to the sheriff.

'Well,' said Tucker, 'if you feel easy about having this fellow in your home, then I shall be off.' He turned to Bridges. 'I hope that you will recollect that this is a decent house and that you must moderate your behaviour. I hope that I am not mistook about you.'

'Leave the poor man alone,' said Mrs Larssen. 'I make no doubt that he and I shall get along just fine. Goodnight to you.'

When the sheriff had gone Mrs Larssen showed Bridges to a neat little room and gave him to understand that food would be upon the table in fifteen minutes and that he had a chance to freshen up first.

Bridges made an effort to make himself look a little cleaner and more respectable. The sheriff had been right, this was a decent house and he felt keenly that his usual free and easy ways would not answer here.

After the allotted time he went down to the kitchen, where the red-and-white gingham tablecloth was set with a finer spread than he had seen in some months.

'You did not need to go to such trouble,' he said, a little embarrassed by the bounty. 'I do not eat a whole lot in general.'

'It is a while since I had company. It is purely a pleasure to prepare food for a guest, especially one who has had such a trying time over the last few hours.'

'Touching upon which,' said Bridges, 'I would not like you to think . . . that . . . which is to say . . . '

'That you strangled that girl?' she enquired coolly. 'I don't think anything of the sort. Neither, I'll wager, does my nephew, or he would not have brought you here.'

'Your nephew? The sheriff is your nephew?'

'Yes, that is so. But enough, I am hungry and so I dare say are you. Will you say grace?'

'I have not spoke a blessing over the table since I was a child,' said Bridges. 'I am not sure that I could find the right words.'

71

Mrs Larssen shot the uncomfortable man an amused glance. 'Give it a try, Mr Bridges. I am sure that the Lord will understand if you are a little out of practice.'

Bridges cleared his throat and then said in a halting voice, 'Lord, we thank you for what you have given us this day. That is to say, I thank Mrs Larssen for what she has done with what you have provided. We have not spoke much in some twenty years and I hope that you have not forgot me. With all your other responsibilities, is what I mean to say. Amen.'

As he finished his impromptu prayer, Bridges was disconcerted to see that Mrs Larssen's eyes had filled with tears. He patted her arm awkwardly, saying, 'There ma'am, don't take on so.'

'Well,' she said, dabbing at her eyes with a pocket handkerchief, 'That didn't go too badly, did it? It is affecting to hear somebody getting to know the Lord again after a long absence. Now tell me about yourself as we eat.'

Bridges gave a rough account of his life on the trail and how he had taken it into his mind to settle down in a town for a spell.

'And how do you find our town, Mr Bridges? Does life here compare favourably with how you find things on the trail?'

'Well ma'am,' said Bridges, 'it does and it doesn't, if you take my meaning. Living in the town is a sight more comfortable than living and working outside, but there are parts of the business that I don't take to.'

'Which parts would those be, Mr Bridges?'

'Well, I don't want to give offence, you understand, but it strikes me as though folks in town are not as open and honest as I have been used to.' He gave a few examples, including the preacher from the church which he had attended.

'Oh him,' she said, when he mentioned the name of the church in question. 'Yes, I take your point well enough there. As for the rest of what you might take as hypocrisy, we are strangely situated in Stockton. You must not judge all towns by the example of this one place.'

'I am not sure that I take your meaning, ma'am. How so are you strangely situated?'

'Have you not noticed,' said Mrs Larssen, 'The uncommon number of saloons and other . . . establishments which we boast? Our whole, entire town is dependent upon the money from people like yourself. True, there is employment on the railroads and in the stockyards, but in general, all of us earn our incomes from you cowboys. We rent you rooms, sell you liquor, feed you, provide you with clothes and a hundred other things.

'We try to turn a blind eye to some of the goings on and pretend that they are nothing to do with us, but they are. I am talking of some of the more . . . liberal saloons.'

Bridges asked hesitantly, 'Do you

mean the places where girls . . . are a little free?'

'I'm talking about brothels and saloons, yes. Heavens man, don't look so shocked. I'm a widow, not a maiden lady. Truth is, everybody is pleased to have the cathouses, because with a set of single men getting liquored-up regularly, it stands to reason that they will want to cut free a little and let the badger loose from time to time.

'If there were not those girls down at the hurdy-gurdy house and other places, then those boys would be pestering the daughters and wives of respectable citizens. That would set the cat among the pigeons and so we make out that we don't know about prostitution and such like. All that money finds its way into our pockets too in the end.

'You could say that Stockton is based upon prostitution, gambling and the sale of liquor. I don't wonder you think us a set of hypocrites.'

Bridges sat and digested this for a space. He had only thought of 'fallen women' in the past as abstractions, never thinking about how they came to 'fall' or what advantage there might be to others in the process.

As though reading his thoughts, Mrs Larssen cut in, saying, 'You know there are many virtuous women in this town who are grateful for what those girls get up to. It keeps them safe and allows them to continue virtuous.'

'I had not seen the thing in that light. You mean that you all pretend not to know that much of the money in your town is from gambling and suchlike, so that you may carry on being respectable?'

'Ha! Yes, that is one way of putting it.'

'I don't know,' said Bridges, 'but that I don't prefer the way of it when I am among men who do not put on such airs. When I ride with men on the trail, one might say that he wishes to get drunk when we hit town or that he feels the need for a woman. There is no show or acting about them. Would you be minding if I was to be getting to bed now, ma'am? I have a long day tomorrow.'

As he lay in bed, Bridges turned over what he had been told in his mind. It all went some way to explain why he felt that there were too many lies and deceits being practised in this town; why he longed to be back with folk who just said straight out what they were thinking and feeling.

★   ★   ★

The next day, after having a pleasant breakfast with Mrs Larssen, Bridges went into the town to see what was what. He knew now for sure that Kirby was mixed up in this affair, along with the fellow with the mustache who was evidently known as the 'colonel'. It was also a fair bet that Marion knew something about things as well. *If I cannot make something of all that*, he thought to himself, *then I am getting old and silly.*

While he was walking slowly along

Main Street, trying to figure out what his first port of call should be, a nattily dressed man wearing, of all unlikely things in that town, a derby, fell into step alongside him.

'Tell me now,' said the smart-looking fellow, 'would I happen to be addressing the man as worked in the Yellow Rose until a day or two back?'

Bridges stopped dead, saying, 'That you are. But you will find it better policy to come straight out with what you wish to know. I do not have a deal of patience for fooling around and foxing with folk.'

The fellow chuckled in delight. 'A man after my own heart. Well then, I am an officer with the detective branch of the New York police and I am here to make some enquiries. I'd not wish to go into too much detail in a public place like this, where we might be seen. If you would take a stroll with me up past the railroad tracks, we might do each other some good. Phelps is my name. Cornelius Phelps.'

When the two of them had walked a hundred yards or so and were out of earshot of any passers-by, the man in the derby stopped and said to Bridges,

'I have here in my pocket a likeness of a man we are interested in. Look here.'

He drew from his pocket a small photographic image, taken in a studio by the look of it. A sullen and ill-favoured man was standing next to a pot of aspidistras and doing his best to smile.

'I mind that I have seen this fellow before,' said Bridges cautiously. 'But you have yet to tell me what your interest in him might be.'

'This is a very big case on which I am working,' said the other man importantly. It was clear that he was hoping to impress Bridges with his big talk and make him feel flattered that a police officer from New York would be seeking his assistance.

'I cannot go into great detail, for obvious reasons, but I can tell you that we have been ordered by the President himself to make this matter a priority. It affects other nations.'

All this sounded to Bridges like so much flannel.

'Let us rightly understand each other,' he said, 'I do not care at all about other nations. I have my own concerns and don't suppose that those there 'other nations' of which you speak would be much bothered about my troubles. What are you asking of me?'

'Do you know anything of the man in that picture?' asked the other bluntly.

'I have seen him around, both in the Yellow Rose and elsewhere. I have cause to think that he is known as 'the colonel'. Is that what you wish to know?'

'We already know all that. I have been in the Yellow Rose, under a different guise. We in the detective branch are used to changing our appearance when it is needful. I want more than this. Do you know who his contacts are in this town?'

'You ask a good many questions,' observed Bridges. 'Let me try one. Are your enquiries aimed towards men who are in the custom of taking young girls anywhere against their will or aught of that sort?'

The other gave a start. 'You do know something about this business. Out with it, man; you best not fool with me! Tell me what you know.'

'Tell me,' said Bridges. 'Does the sheriff know of your presence in town? By which I mean, do you have the authority of a lawman, or are these questions of yours just the same as those of a private citizen?'

This was such a shrewd question that the man glanced sharply at Bridges, thinking that he must have misjudged the man.

'That is what they call a debatable point,' he said, after considering for a few seconds. 'Which is to say that he knows I am here, but that my warrant does not extend this far from New York.'

81

'Yes,' said Bridges, nodding in a satisfied way.

'That is how I read the case. You have no more right to ask me questions than I have you. Still and all, that does not mean that we cannot work together towards the same end. It is just as well though that we both know where we stand. Otherwise, you might start trying to boss me about and buffalo me. That would not answer.'

The man from New York stared at the slow-talking cowboy with a new respect. It was not often that he had been pricked and deflated so skilfully and he felt a grudging admiration for the man who had done this.

'Well,' he said, 'having got that little misunderstanding resolved, where do we stand? Will you assist me? I know you were working in the Yellow Rose and I have also heard of your recent difficulties. I would think that you would be as keen as me to put one over on Kirby or the colonel.'

'That is so. What do you suggest?'

'I have to go away this afternoon. I shall be back tomorrow. If you could think about this while I am gone? Without giving away too much, I will tell you that the job I am on is looking for a very large room, maybe almost as big as the bar-room in a saloon. It might be in a private house or on a ranch. There would need to be large windows with a lot of light for the place. If you can find anywhere of that sort, then we can work from there.'

'Will you tell me no more than this?' asked Bridges.

'Not for now. But you are perhaps better placed than me to know where such a location might be found. I will be open with you and say that Sheriff Tucker is not very pleased to have me in town. He will not help me. Some men are like that, wanting only to rule their little kingdom and giving no thought to the greater good.'

'By which,' said Bridges, 'I understand that your nose is all put out of joint because he did not see a city detective as being of more importance than a small-town sheriff. Yes, I see that well enough.'

'That's nothing to the purpose,' said the man from New York. 'Where are you currently staying?' Bridges told him and it was agreed that they would meet the next day.

After they had parted, Bridges walked round town for a spell, straightening things out in his mind a little. There could be no doubt that both his former boss, Kirby, and the man known as the colonel were up to their necks in some species of mischief which was serious enough to attract the attention of the police from hundreds of miles away.

This ruled out such day-to-day misdemeanours as prostitution or bootlegging. The police in New York would hardly concern themselves with a man running a cathouse in a little cow town like Stockton. No, there must be some bigger picture, which he could not see.

Now, he was so deep in thought that

Bridges did not at first notice how those he passed were reacting to him. He was drawn from his reveries by the sound of a man he had just passed hawking and spitting. He turned to see that this man had deliberately spat after him as they passed.

'Hey feller,' said Bridges in an amiable tone of voice, 'you might want to be a bit careful where you're spitting.'

The man, who had as Bridges later surmised, been looking for an excuse to start trouble, came up to Bridges right quick, saying,

'What did you say, you murdering son of a bitch?'

'I said you might want to watch where you are spitting.'

Now Bridges had been in enough rough-houses in his time to be up to all the tricks that men got up to when they were aiming to get the drop on an opponent before a fight actually began. So when the man in front of him leaned forward a shade, Bridges bent his head down, tucking his chin into his chest.

So it was that when the man swung his forehead down sharply, intending to bang it into Bridges's nose, the ploy miscarried. Instead, he found Bridges jumping slightly, so the top of his head made hard and painful contact with the other man's nose instead. Bridges followed this up with a careless but extremely hard blow to the fellow's stomach, which left him doubled up in agony. He fell to the sidewalk, rocking to and fro. Whereupon Chris Bridges delivered himself of the following words of advice:

'Next time you want to fight a man, you challenge him first. I cannot be doing with that sort of sneaky attack, where you start in on a fellow without giving him a chance to defend himself.'

He turned to the passers-by who had stopped to watch. 'I do not know if any of you think that I had a hand in the death of that poor child, but it is nothing of the sort. Else why would your sheriff have freed me?

'Howsoever, if any of you men feel that you wish to take matters into your own hands, then you may confront me either now or later. I am ready for all comers.'

He found no takers. As he stood there, looking round to see if anybody would accept his challenge, there was a shout from the other side of the street.

'Hey, Bridges, you old bastard!'

Riding up was an old friend of his who had hitched up with another cattle-driving outfit. He had not seen hide nor hair of Tommy Clayton for two years or so.

'Well, Clayton,' said Bridges as the younger man rode up to him, 'this is a sight for sore eyes and no mistake. It is some little while since we met. How is the world treating you?'

Clayton was a good fifteen years younger than Bridges, but the two men had got along pretty well when they worked together. It was good to see a friend and Bridges was more pleased at the chance encounter than he cared to show.

'I have had a trying time of it lately,' he said. 'But that don't signify. What's happening?'

'We brought in a herd this morning and now we are for painting the town red. Will you join us?'

'That depends. What have you in mind?'

'First off is where a few of the boys have it in mind to visit the Golden Eagle. You most likely know it, it is a hurdy house.'

'Yes, I will make up one of a party going in that direction.'

The two of them agreed to meet up later that day.

★　★　★

Now although Bridges had no particular wish to talk to or even see Marion Finch again, it looked to him as though she would certainly be able to fill in one or two pieces of the puzzle with which he was grappling. At the very least, she could tell him why she had told such lies about him and who had put her up to it.

He still felt sore about this, but if it would get him further advanced in his quest, he would just bite his tongue and let her explain her actions; that is if she was inclined in that direction, which was open to doubt.

It being around midday, Bridges headed back to Mrs Larssen's, as she had told him to be sure to return for a meal at that time. While they were eating she asked him how long he was planning on staying. Bridges took this as hint that he might not be welcome beyond a certain time, but he was soon corrected on that point.

'You may stay as long as you please from my side,' she told him. 'I was wondering only whether you had any idea yet about how to proceed with clearing your name?'

'I think that I have,' said Bridges. He told her about the New York policeman and also his plan to go to the hurdy-gurdy house that night. For all that she was a God-fearing and respectable widow woman, Mrs Larssen seemed to be very up to date with all the affairs of the town, even those of the most dubious and shady nature.

'You mean the Golden Eagle?' she said. 'That is one of those places which I mentioned last night, that is to say it has a good number of young women who, some might say are no better than they ought to be. You say that you went out once with one of the girls?'

'I accompanied her to the musical theatre, but that was the limit of our acquaintance,' said Bridges, a little stiffly.

'Don't take on. I was not hinting at anything more. Do you think that she will give you any news of those whom you are hoping to bring to justice?'

'She knows something, that is for sure.'

'Tell me,' said Mrs Larssen, 'and don't take it amiss; are you doing this for the sake of that murdered girl or to clear your own name?'

'Both!' was the prompt answer.

★ ★ ★

At about five that afternoon Bridges smartened himself up and went into the centre of town to meet Tommy Clayton.

'What's this I hear about you fetching up in jail?' was how his friend greeted him.

'Yes, there was some unpleasantness of that sort,' admitted Bridges. 'It is for that reason that I am keen to visit the Golden Eagle, which is not an establishment I have ever been to.'

'You're a strange one, Bridges,' said Clayton. 'You mean you never paid for a girl?'

'I would not think of it. I like women well enough, but I am not so desperate for their company that I would pay out cash money.'

'It ain't exactly their company that men pays for,' said Clayton. 'I take it that we cannot visit the Yellow Rose for a bite to eat before going by the hurdy?'

'It would sit ill with me to spend money in that place,' said Bridges. 'Not to mention where I would very likely not be served there.'

After a little discussion, they settled upon an eating-house near the Golden Eagle.

Clayton knew Bridges well enough not to entertain the least doubt about the man's innocence of the crime for which he had been arrested. Anybody who rode with Bridges for a time would know that he was as honest and straight as they came. He might be a mite old-fashioned in his views on life, but he was definitely not a man who would harm a woman, no matter what the circumstances. He had that almost superstitious reverence and respect for females that was once common on the frontier.

'You say that the girl as told such lies about you is working in the hurdy?' asked Clayton. 'Would you like me and a couple of the boys to fetch her out so that we can ask her some questions without anybody interfering?'

'No,' said Bridges, appalled. 'It is not to be thought of. I shall find a chance to catch her alone and see what she will say to me. I beg that you don't involve yourself in the matter. I mean it, Clayton, leave well alone.'

His friend shrugged. 'Well, if you say so. I reckon that between you, me and three or four of the boys from the outfit I am riding with, it would not take us long to ferret out the truth.'

'That is as maybe. I prefer to use my own methods.'

5

Despite being familiar with Stockton, Bridges had never visited any of the less salubrious drinking places. He restricted himself to saloons like the Yellow Rose, in which the clientele were exclusively masculine. He looked around the Golden Eagle appraisingly.

It was a little smaller than the Yellow Rose, with two or three important differences. First off, instead of a faro table and billiards table there was a piano. Secondly, there were a good number of girls. You could dance with these girls for fifty cents, but if you did, then it was expected that you would buy them a drink afterwards.

Although these drinks were poured from bottles with imposing labels, suggesting that they contained the most rare and costly liqueurs, in fact there was nothing more intoxicating than cold tea or coloured sugar water in them. The last thing the management wanted was their girls getting so drunk that they were unable to dance.

In addition to the girls, there were three or four tough and capable-looking men whose role was evidently similar to that which Bridges had held in the Yellow Rose. They watched to see if any of the men were making a nuisance of themselves or not dancing with the girls enough or buying them drinks. They weeded out these 'deadbeats' ruthlessly and woe betide any customer who was not dancing at least twice an hour.

Clayton and his friends were having a great time. It was generally understood that most of the girls here were for sale, but that you had to negotiate terms with them privately. The owners of the hurdy house did not want to get closed down and so avoided giving the open appearance of a brothel. Their money came from the inflated price of the drinks and half the money that the girls were paid for their dancing, rather than prostitution.

Bridges chose one agreeable-looking young woman and asked her if she would dance with him.

'Sure,' she said, 'I'll dance with Satan if he coughs up the fifty cents.'

'Have you worked here long?' asked Bridges, as they moved round the floor.

'Maybe a couple of months,' said the girl. 'Why?'

'Just making conversation.'

'Well don't,' said the girl tartly. 'My life is my business. You paid for a dance, not the chance to hear my life history.'

'Ain't you the charmer!' said Bridges sourly. He was duly gouged for the price of the shot of sugar water the girl chose after the dance was ended.

It was just then that he caught sight of Marion arriving for the evening. She saw him at the same moment and he marked how she started with surprise to find him there in her place of work. However, she recovered herself and nodded to him as though there was nothing wrong.

Bridges sat down for a while and watched Marion dancing with a couple of men. He had to time the thing right. The rule in the house was that the girls could not decline a dance if asked. The management did not want to see even the most repulsive and unattractive of men deprived of their chance to be cheated of their money while patronizing their establishment. Just as she was being handed her overpriced drink at the bar, Bridges pounced.

'May I have the pleasure of the next dance, miss?' he asked politely and in the hearing of one of those running the place. Given the circumstances, the girl could hardly decline.

'Very well,' she said ungraciously.

Once they were on the dance floor Bridges said, 'Do not imagine that it is your personality that caused me to ask for this dance. I want to know who put you up to telling those lies about me?'

'I'm surprised you should ask,' she said pertly. 'I would have thought you might have guessed.'

'Well then, I guess they call him the colonel.'

'You have wasted fifty cents,' said Marion, 'Seeing as how you already knew the answer.'

'So it was him. The same as I threw out of that musical theatre the night before last?'

'You have it all figured out. I'm sure I don't know what you want of me.'

'What I want of you is to know why you felt that you had to do as this 'colonel' told you. Does he have a hold over you?'

'You might say so,' said the girl wearily. 'He is my protector.'

'Protector?' said Bridges, 'What do you mean?'

'You really are fresh and green, ain't you, for all that you are old enough to be my father? He arranges who I screw with and suchlike. There now, I have shocked you.'

'Surprised, not shocked. Are you the only girl he looks after in that way?'

'No, of course not. He has other

concerns as well, but that brings in a good income to him.'

'Well, you are being obliging enough, I will allow. Are you not afraid to talk so openly?'

'No, I have said nothing that is new to anybody here.'

The dance was nearly over. 'What is his connection with Kirby over at the Yellow Rose?' asked Bridges.

'I use a room there for business. The colonel arranges that. Also, he and Kirby have some other project going, but I know nothing of that. And I am sorry about telling lies to the sheriff. You are a decent man.'

Marion led him to the bar after the dance had finished and he paid a dollar and a half for a small glass of cold, sweetened tea for her to sip. As he made to move off, she did something unexpected, which was to lean over and kiss him on the cheek. Then she blushed and turned away.

While he sat with Clayton and his friends, Bridges wondered why Marion had been so free about the facts of the case. He eventually decided that it was because she had not told him anything which he could not have worked out himself or found out from others. He had already known that the man known as 'the colonel' must have told her to lie to the sheriff. It was also clear that this fellow and Kirby had some business going together. As to the fact that the colonel ran Marion and some other girls as prostitutes, Bridges guessed that that was by way of being an open secret anyway.

He had got all this neatly figured, when a rough looking cowboy deliberately barged into him where he was sitting minding his own busines, and then said,

'Hey buster, you have made me spill my drink!'

This was so outrageous that Bridges smiled, whereupon the man said,

'You think this is funny? Know how to use that gun you're wearing? Maybe you'd like to settle this outside?'

Bridges stood up, and almost at exactly the same moment Clayton and his two friends also got to their feet. Clayton said to the man who was trying to start a fight,

'You start it with one of us, you take us all on.'

'It's OK, Clayton,' said Bridges. 'It's real good of you, but I don't think me and this fellow are going to fall out. Please, resume your seats and he and I will thrash this matter out.'

The three others sat down at Bridges's bidding, but continued to glare at the stranger. As for Bridges, he felt that this was an opportunity to pursue his enquiries a little further. There could be no doubt that this man had been instructed to pick a quarrel with him on any pretext and then probably lead him to his death.

He said to the man, 'Come on, my friend, let's talk this over outside, peaceable like.' He saw the look of satisfaction pass fleetingly across the man's face.

The two men left the Golden Eagle, Bridges following the other. The second that they were out of the door, Bridges grabbed ahold of the fellow from behind without any warning. He forced the man's arm up behind his back with one hand and plucked the fellow's pistol from its holster with the other, tossing it to one side.

Then, having disarmed him, he marched the man round the corner of the building into a stinking alleyway which drunks often used to relieve themselves. He pushed the man's face up against the wooden wall with considerable force and then said,

'I do not in general hold with attacking a man from behind in this way, without warning. Howsoever, I have an idea that you were leading me into a trap and so do not feel guilty about it on this occasion.'

The man said nothing, biding his time and seeing what would chance.

Bridges continued, 'Now I don't believe that you were expecting a fair fight. I think you wanted the appearance of one, which is why you made sure that we were seen going out of that pest hole together. What was it to be? Somebody up on a roof with a rifle, was it? Well?' He pushed the man's face harder against the wall, indicating that he was prepared to play it as rough as the fellow wanted.

'Yes,' said the man. 'There is someone waiting up on the roof opposite. It was thought that in the dark, you could be shot and it would look like I had drawn down on you quicker than you was able.'

'So that nobody would enquire further, was that the game?'

'Yes. You have pissed off some people in this town. It was hoped that you would just dig up after you was freed from jail.'

'I do not care for scurvy tricks of that nature,' said Bridges. 'I am more than half minded to kill you, right where we stand. Tell me why I should not?'

'I will tell you what I know if you

spare my life,' said the man, his voice rising an octave in fear as Bridges drew and cocked his piece, pressing it to the other's ear.

'Talk then, or it is all up with you.'

'There is some racket going on in the town that is run by somebody known as 'the colonel'. You know who I mean?'

'I know,' said Bridges.

'Couple of nights ago you humiliated the colonel in front of a bunch of folk and then stepped into the middle of his operation and fouled it up. He decided to put you out of action.'

'Why did he not just shoot me the other night? Why all that business about setting me forward as a murderer?'

'I think that they worried that you would have found something out from the girl. They wanted her and you dead. Some of the colonel's men were trying to stir things up to have you lynched. It would have ended the matter neatly, without too many questions being asked and answered.'

Bridges's blood was fairly boiling to

hear this weasel talk so calmly of fixing a terrible crime on him, to say nothing of the death of the girl herself. He said, 'What is this racket you talk of?'

'I don't know and that's God's honest truth. I act for the colonel in little matters such as this. He only calls upon me when he has need, I do not work for him regular like some. All I know is that it is a big thing, calculated to make a number of people wealthy.'

'Is it something in the way of whores and so on?'

'No, I do not think so. I couldn't say. They don't trust me.'

'No,' said Bridges. 'And it is not to be wondered at. Be off now, before I change my mind and shoot you.'

Bridges went back into the hurdy house and assured Clayton that he was fine. After thanking the others heartily for their help, he bid them a good night. He left with his hand ready on the hilt of his pistol, but there was no trouble. Perhaps the man with the rifle had been stood down after Bridges's chat with the one who tried to lure him into the street. He went home and after bidding goodnight to Mrs Larssen, slept soundly.

6

Bridges woke early the next day, and before getting dressed he lay thinking about what he should do that day. He recollected that he was due to see the policeman from New York again and then remembered what had been said about this project: that Kirby and the colonel were involved in needing a large room with plenty of light. What the hell was that all about? Nevertheless, it was a good start to things if he could track down such a location in or near the town, before hitching up with the man from New York.

He fell half-asleep again after running over all the things he was going to do, but then woke with a start as he realized that the answer to that question about the large room might already be known to him.

At breakfast, Mrs Larssen was

disposed to be chatty. Although he was raring to be out and doing, Bridges thought that it would be mighty discourteous to cut the old lady short and so he talked of this and that with her for nigh on an hour.

The fellow from New York had said that he was searching for somewhere with a big room, something like to the size of a bar-room, that had plenty of light. It was the thought of bar-rooms that put it into Bridges's head that he knew just where this mysterious room could be. After leaving Mrs Larssen's house, he went into town and took a turn around the Yellow Rose.

One of the things that had surprised him when he was staying at the Yellow Rose was that the upstairs quarters were extremely cramped. It was easy enough to see how much space there should be on the first and second floors of the building, just by looking at the size of the bar-room and kitchen. Yet when you went up the stairs to the next floor, all you came to was a stubby little corridor containing three rooms running off it like a hotel.

Carrying on up the stairs took you to the top floor. There again, there were only a few small rooms. There was the room where Bridges had been living and some others filled with lumber, but that was all. Kirby didn't live over the shop and he had never heard of anybody else living on the premises, so there was a lot of space unaccounted for.

It being so early, it did not seem likely to Bridges that Kirby would be around the saloon yet, and so he felt free to walk round the building, which occupied a lot right smack-bang in the middle of town.

Bridges paced out the measurements and then tried to calculate how much space was taken up on the other floors by rooms which he knew about. A space about three quarters of the size of the ground floor bar-room was missing on the upper floors, which would probably be what the man from the detective branch was looking for.

He had never had occasion to go to the back alley running behind the Yellow Rose, but he found that there was a back door, which he had never seen.

He knew that there was no corresponding door in the kitchen at the rear of the bar and so it was a fair guess that this outside door led to a staircase of some sort, leading to the concealed parts of the upper storeys of the saloon. What the hell is he doing there? thought Bridges to himself.

The only thing was that the New York policeman had also said that this big room would need a lot of light from large windows, and that was not at all the case with the back wall of the Yellow Rose, which sported only three tiny windows of the sort that would let in very little light. Bridges wondered if he could get a better view of the place if he could get on to one of the nearby rooftops.

The Yellow Rose was the highest

building bar one in the centre of town. The only building of around the same height was the telegraph office, which had offices above it. It did not take Bridges long to find that a fire escape led up to the roof of this place.

The sheriff would not perhaps be best pleased if he heard about Bridges clambering over the roof of the telegraph office, but that could not be helped. He picked his way carefully across the roof, which creaked ominously beneath his feet. He tried to keep to the edge, near the walls where he would be putting less strain on the tarred wood of which the roof was made. It would be mighty embarrassing to fall through the roof and land in somebody's office! Moving carefully in this way, he eventually found himself crouching next to a chimney stack, a little above the level of the Yellow Rose's roof.

Bridges smiled, pleased with himself. He could not get a right good view, but he could see enough of the rooftop to see that the hidden part of the saloon was covered with an array of skylights, which would let in as much light as the biggest windows. This was, for a bet, the room that he was looking for.

What it all meant, though, was still a complete mystery. Not a brothel, that was for sure. Whoever heard of a secret brothel or one that needed plenty of light? He was probably the only man in town, apart from those involved in the business, who knew the location of this strange enterprise.

While he was reflecting in a satisfied way on his own cleverness in this matter he heard a sound behind him and turned to find Sheriff Tucker tip-toeing gingerly across the roof towards him.

'I might have guessed,' said the sheriff, in a resigned tone. 'Every bit of trouble in this town lately seems to have you at the centre of it, Bridges. How is that?'

Bridges shrugged. 'I don't rightly know. I try to make myself inconspicuous-like.'

'Mind telling me what you're doing up here? I was told that somebody was about to rob the telegraph office, but I should have known better. I mean it, what are you about?'

'I was kind of staking out the Yellow Rose. Just to keep an eye on it, if you take my meaning.'

'I don't. What do you mean, staking it out? What do you hope to achieve by this?' The sheriff stared at the back of the Yellow Rose. He apparently saw nothing to rouse his suspicions, because he turned back to Bridges.

'Come on, let's get down to the street. I wanted to speak to you anyway, so in a way this has saved me the bother of hunting for you.'

Down at street level, the sheriff and Bridges stopped in an empty lot to exchange a few words.

'I hear from Mrs Larssen,' began Tucker, before Bridges interrupted, saying:

'You mean your aunt?'

'Yeah, so what if she's my aunt? What the hell's that got to do with the price of sugar?'

'Nothing at all,' said Bridges, unabashed. 'I just found it curious, a fellow like you having such a kind and caring person as an aunt.'

'Bridges, you came close to getting your neck stretched a day or two back. Do not cause me to repent of having released you from custody. Maybe we can get back to the matter in hand?'

'Sure, you go right ahead.'

'Thank you. I hear that you have met or had some sort of dealings with a man called Phelps who works for the detective branch of the police in New York.'

'We have spoke, yes.'

'Do you know what he is after? He was a mite cagey when talking to me.'

'He says that some crime is being committed here, but he did not say what. He strikes me as being very full of himself.'

'That was my impression of him as

well. He tried to put on a front with me, but soon found that it was not working. Let me speak plainly: do you know what he is after?'

Bridges did not answer for a second or two. Then he said, 'All I understand is that this has something to do with Kirby. He would not vouchsafe to me the nature of the thing he is looking into.' This was all true, although not the complete truth and it salved Bridges's conscience not to have to tell a direct lie about the business.

'There is something going on in this town that I should know about and it sits ill with me that I have not the least idea what it might be. The death of that girl is all of a piece with it, but I can't make out at all what they wanted her for. I don't think this is white slaving or anything of that sort. I believe that they were intending as they said to return her to her mother's home after she had performed some service for them. What that might be is beyond me.'

Bridges was looking into the distance

and did not, to the sheriff, appear to be taking note of what was being said.

'If you would favour me with your attention for a few seconds, Bridges,' he said with heavy politeness, but Bridges cut in sharply, saying;

'That man yonder, him as is walking across the way there towards the street. I am certain-sure that he is one of those as had charge of young Ellie Cartwright.'

'The hell it is,' exclaimed the sheriff. 'Are you sure?'

'That I am.'

'Well then, we best see what he has to say for himself.'

The man whom Bridges had indicated was strolling casually from the back of the Yellow Rose, looking as though he was going to walk round the back of the neighbouring building and so on to Main Street. It occurred to Bridges later that he might very well have come out of that back door to the Yellow Rose. At any rate, he and Sheriff Tucker began tailing the fellow, who looked behind him, realized that he was being followed and broke into a run.

'After him!' cried the sheriff and the pair of them pursued the fleeing man on to Main Street. There matters took an unexpected and alarming turn when the man drew the pistol he was wearing at his hip and fired a couple of shots at them. One of the balls passed within a few inches of Bridges's left ear, so close that he heard it buzz by like an angry bee.

'Shit,' said Bridges and drew his own piece, firing back at the man.

'Don't kill him,' said the sheriff urgently. 'I want him alive so that we can unravel this thread once and for all.'

In dime novels it is the work of a moment to wing a man or shoot the gun right out of his hand. In real life, though, it is quite another thing. The fellow ran along the street, turning and firing every few seconds. He was trying to reload on the move, when one of the sheriff's bullets hit him right in the back of his head, blowing out half his brains.

'Goddamn!' said the sheriff. 'I just knew that would happen.' He and Bridges reached the man, who was already dead, although still twitching a little. Fortunately, the shot had not disfigured his face, which was still intact, although splashed with blood and particles of grey matter. Some of those who had thrown themselves to the ground to avoid getting shot were now drifting over to see what was what.

'Anybody know this man?' asked the sheriff.

'I might,' said a middle-aged man. 'Can I come a little closer? I don't see too good without my glasses.'

'You think at a time like this I want to hear a list of your medical infirmities?' asked Tucker. 'Get as close as you please if you can tell me who he is and where he lives.'

The fussy little man approached the corpse, saying, 'Lordy, there's bits of brain matter all over the place. I do not want to get it on my shoes.'

He crouched down by the body, peering hard at the face, before saying, 'Yes, it is as I thought. His given name is Elroy and he lives up at the barn on the Richardson spread. South of here, you know.'

'Yeah,' said the sheriff. 'I know the place. What do you mean, he lives in the barn? That is a strange circumstance.'

'He rented it out from old man Richardson about a year ago. He said he wanted it for storage, although Lord knows what he was keeping there. I heard some weeks ago that he stays there in the barn when he is in the area. That is all I know.'

Sheriff Tucker turned to Bridges. 'And this is without a doubt the fellow you saw the other night holding that girl?'

'Yes, that is certain. I cannot say that I am sorry to see him dead, thinking on what he and his partner must have done. I am only sorry that it was not my bullet which took him.'

'That's enough of that talk. We must have a proper reverence for the dead,' said the sheriff, a little shocked at this callous attitude.

'Are we going up to this Richardson's place?' enquired Bridges.

'There is no 'we' in the case,' said the sheriff sharply. 'I am going up there, but I do not need you to come. You are not a deputy or nothing like it. Do not start getting above yourself, Bridges; you are still officially a suspect in a murder case.'

'You would rather I worked on my own to find out what is going on?' asked Bridges in a meek sounding voice. 'Well, perhaps you are right. I will bid you good day.' He began to walk off.

'Not so hasty. I do not propose to have you roaming around and muddying up all the trails. If you are set upon it, you may accompany me to this barn. Just set mind to who is in charge, that is all that I am saying.'

'Why, Sheriff,' said Bridges. 'That is you, of course.'

★ ★ ★

Eli Richardson's farm was four miles out of town. His barn was set back behind some trees. He had built a new one a couple of years previously and had been delighted when a stranger had walked on to his property one day and offered to rent the disused barn.

'Tell me,' said Tucker, 'You did not think anything odd about somebody quite unknown to you walking in and asking to rent your barn?'

Richardson was a peppery old man who did not take to being asked questions.

'Odd? What do you mean, odd? What should I have done? Come to town and ask for a permit to let out my own property?'

The sheriff stared at the old fellow balefully.

'Do not adopt that tone when speaking to me. I will not have it. Do you want me to start poking round your farm and looking for trouble? I tell you now, when I start looking for cause to arrest somebody or make their lives a misery, I generally find it. Just carry on down your present road and that is what I shall do.'

Old man Richardson was sobered by this.

'No, no, I do not want us to fall out. I have never had problems with the law yet and I do not want to start at my age.'

'Well then, suppose you tell me about this fellow and your barn.'

'He came here about a year, year and a half ago. Said he was starting up some business in town and needed somewhere to store materials. It was something in the manufacturing line and he didn't want folk prying into what he was using. He told me that he did not want all the things delivered to an address in town because it would invite questions.'

While he was relating this to Tucker, Bridges marked that Eli Richardson was watching the sheriff with a cunning, sidelong look as though he had something to hide. He wondered if Tucker was aware of this, but needn't have worried.

'Something in the manufacturing line, you say,' asked the sheriff pleasantly. 'And what did you make of that?'

Richardson shrugged. 'Didn't make nothing at all of it. None of my affair, I was just renting him some space to store stuff.'

'In plain language, you thought he was a moonshiner. You guessed that he had set up a still in your barn and was bootlegging liquor, probably to the Indians. Isn't that about the strength of it?'

The old man shrugged again, repeating, 'It was none of my affair.'

'I tell you now,' said the sheriff, 'if something illegal has been taking place on your land, that is precisely your affair. Let's have a look-see in this famous barn and find what is in there.'

'I don't have the key. He fitted a big shiny new padlock soon as he took the place.'

'You got a crowbar or even a length of metal?' asked Bridges. 'I will engage to enter the place, lock or no.'

When they bust open the door of the barn, there was nothing at all for Eli Richardson to worry about. There was a camp bed in one corner and a table stacked with glass jars set against one of the walls. There was also a lot of scrap paper and the remains of packing cases, which had been opened, but no indication at all of what might have been in those cases. The glass jars, roughly gallon size, were filled with white crystals. There were fifteen of them altogether.

'What the hell is this stuff?' said the sheriff.

Bridges was poking around in the litter on the floor and came up with a printed invoice.

'I reckon this here is for those jars,'

he said. He handed the piece of paper to the sheriff.

'Sodium thiosulfate? What is that? Has either of you heard of this?'

Richardson, who had been enormously relieved to find that his barn had not been used for bootlegging or gun-running, chipped in helpfully at this point.

'It is bleach. You can use it to sterilize stuff. We had a batch once to clean all the pails and so on in the dairy which I once ran here.'

'Something is not right here,' said the sheriff. 'Why would a man go to all this trouble to hide the fact that he was buying bleach? There is more to this than meets the eye.'

Irritated that he was no further forward on getting to the bottom of things, he decided to vent his frustration on Richardson.

'As for you, old man, it is perfectly plain to me that you suspicioned that some illegal activity was being conducted on your land. The next time somebody approaches you with a peculiar proposition of this sort, you just report it to me, you hear what I tell you, now?'

'Sure, Sheriff, I'll report it to you. I will be sure to mind that in the future.'

As they left, Richardson called after them.

'There's one more thing I can tell you. I did not recall it to mind until now. Every so often, the fellow Elroy, who had this barn, would rent animals from me.'

The sheriff turned back and went over to Richardson. 'What's this? What are you talking about, rented animals?'

'Just as I say. He would borrow a sheep or calf or sometimes a dog and then take them off for a spell. Sometimes he kept them overnight. They were not hurt when he brought them back.'

'What was he doing with them?'

'I don't know. I did not ask.'

'You have less curiosity than any man I ever met before in the whole course of my life,' said Sheriff Tucker. 'Be sure that you ask a few more questions the next time you have somebody staying here or you will end up in difficulties one of these fine days. I tell you now, I am not at all satisfied with the way that you have concealed what may be a felony. Remember it in the future.'

Bridges and the sheriff rode back to town, neither one of them feeling like talking much. Tucker was feeling foxed and bewildered at these new developments, while Bridges was feeling a quiet satisfaction that every new event made it more and more obvious to everybody that he had been caught up in the middle of a situation which was not of his making. Once this thing had been completely exposed, there would be nobody in Stockton who still thought that he had had a hand in Ellie's death. He could then weigh things up and decide where his life was going next.

As things stood he had not found the experience of living in a town as being a very pleasant or agreeable one. There were worse things than being cold and working long hours out in the open and, truth to tell, he was beginning to think that he had taken the wrong road when he stayed here rather than heading back to Texas.

7

Back at Mrs Larssen's house Bridges lay on the bed, having carefully removed his boots first. He had arranged to see Phelps later that afternoon, but before he met up with the man, he wished to have everything clear in his own mind. He had begged a sheet of writing paper from the widow Larssen and began laboriously writing a list.

Bridges was not a good penman, seldom having need to write anything much. In fact it was not uncommon for him to go six months at a stretch without picking up pen and paper. This is what he wrote:

1. The Yellow Rose has a big, well-lit room which nobody much knows about. The policeman from New York is looking for just such a

place and says that the President of the USA is interested in this matter.

2. Kirby and the colonel are up to something illegal which makes a lot of money.

3. Whatever this project is, girls, animals and a lot of bleach are involved.

Having written all this down, Bridges read through his list and shook his head, utterly baffled. What the hell would anybody be needing huge amounts of bleach for? What had sheep to do with the business?

The whole thing was a regular conundrum to which he despaired of finding an answer. Perhaps he could just leave town now, since it must be clear to most folk by now that he was not answerable for the girl's death? He knew though that he had promised to protect that child and had failed to do so.

Whatever anybody else believed or

did not believe, he knew that he had to bring to justice those who had harmed Ellie Cartwright. He would not be able to look at his face in the mirror each morning when he shaved unless he ensured that all those who had had a hand in the murder were brought to justice, one way or another.

Under his first list, he drew a line and then wrote:

1. Find a way to see what is in that room over the Yellow Rose.
2. Pump Phelps for information.
3. Ask Marion where the colonel lives.

Exhausted by all this thinking and writing, he decided to walk into town and see what chanced there before he met the New York policeman. He did not for a moment suppose that the President himself had the least interest in this affair, but he also guessed that it was big enough for Phelps to have his boss breathing down his neck and urging him to bring in solid results. It would be a question of trading information with Phelps to see who knew what.

At the back of his mind, Bridges was fairly sure that whatever the outcome of all this, he was going to wind up killing either Kirby or this colonel. They seemed likely to be the ones ultimately responsible not only for the death of the child, but also for trying to fix the atrocious crime on Bridges. There would be a reckoning and it was drawing nigh.

The Golden Eagle was not open for business, but there was activity inside as the owners prepared it for another evening of dancing and drinking. When Bridges walked in one of the men who threw out those not spending enough money shouted at him,

'We ain't open yet. Come back at seven.'

'I am not wanting to dance or nothing,' said Bridges. 'I am looking to find a girl who I have seen here. Her name is Marion.'

'What's it worth?' said the man, for whom enquiries of this sort were probably not a rarity. After some species of bargaining, Bridges handed over a sum of money and in return was given the address of the boarding house where the girl lived.

★　★　★

Marion Finch had shared a room in a run-down and dilapidated house near the stockyard. A slatternly and unkempt woman opened the door to Bridges and showed him into a parlour whose furniture was so filthy that he did not even feel like sitting down.

I reckon I have done all right for myself at Mrs Larssen's house, at least compared with this hole, he thought to himself.

When Marion entered the room she gave every sign of being displeased at finding that it was him.

'Lord, have you not seen enough of

me? What are you wanting now? I do not like having visitors from the hurdy here, it makes it look like I'm a whore or something.'

Bridges said nothing. The girl sighed and then said, 'All right, sit down and tell me what you want. I am busy. Some of us have to work, you know.'

'Him you call the colonel, where might I be finding him?' asked Bridges.

'I cannot tell you anything in that direction. My life would like as not be forfeit.'

'I only want to know the fellow's location.'

'Why?'

'He tried to set me up for a hanging. You don't think that would give him and me something to talk about?'

The girl went to the door and looked out into the hallway. When she came back, she sat right next to Bridges and lowered her voice almost to a whisper.

'If I tell you a thing or two, will you promise to leave me alone?'

'Yes, I will.'

'You have had a rough deal and you are not a bad fellow. I am sorry for my part in it. The colonel does not live in town. He comes here at night mostly. I guess he lives five or six miles from here, leastways that is what I gauge from little things that he has let fall. If you set a watch upon the Golden Eagle, you will be sure to come across him in the end. But sometimes he stays away for weeks. There, that is all I can tell you. Will you now go?'

'You spent a lot of time in the Yellow Rose as far as I am able to recollect. Do you know anything about a secret room there?'

Marion looked genuinely puzzled by the question. 'How's that? A secret room? No, I never heard anything of the sort. I only used one room, you know, and that only for an hour or two. There now, please go.'

Bridges rose to his feet. 'I am obliged to you, Marion. From all that I can collect, you had only a small part in this and none of that related to that girl's

135

death. As far as I am concerned, our dealings are now at an end. I would ask you to turn aside from the path you are on though. I say that as a friend.'

She looked truly touched at this and her eyes became bright, as though she might be on the verge of tears. She said,

'Never you set mind to me. I will do well enough. You take care of your own self, you hear me? Why you will not just leave Stockton is somewhat of a mystery to me.'

'Leave? Why, I have unfinished business to tend to. When that is settled, I will go.'

* * *

There was still an hour to kill before meeting Phelps and Bridges thought that he would take another turn by the Yellow Rose. He was more than half convinced that the man whom the sheriff had shot had come out of the back door to the saloon. He also was sure that this door led up to the space on the upper floors that the New York policeman was so keen to track down.

He didn't think that it would be a smart move to start clambering about on rooftops again. Sheriff Tucker had been quite good about that episode, not pressing him too hard about his reasons for being up there in the first instance, but it would not do to push him further.

Nobody was around and so Bridges stood at the back of the saloon, doing his best to measure the distances by eye. He knew that where that door at the back was corresponded to the kitchen, which he had been in often. He was quite sure that there was no door there leading out back.

Out of interest, he went up to the door and turned the handle. There was a stout lock and, looking at the hinges, Bridges made sure that it opened outwards. It would be no easy matter to break down such a door as this. Whoever had installed it knew his business and was not wanting any intrusions.

He had told Phelps that he would meet him in an eating-house down the street aways. Come to think of it, he was hungry now and he could have a bite to eat while waiting for the city policeman.

Phelps was on time and still wearing that ridiculous derby, which for all his talk of the skill of this detective branch of blending in and being inconspicuous, marked him out like a sore thumb. 'Well,' he said, as soon as he was seated, 'have you any news for me. I am a busy man and there is much happening in this case.'

'I don't recall that you told me the nature of what you call this case,' said Bridges. 'Who or what are you seeking?'

'Like I said, in the first instance I am looking for a large room with plenty of light.'

'Yes,' said Bridges patiently, 'I remember that. But why are you so keen on this? Tell me more about this so-called case of yours.'

'Can't be done. This is police business. Why, I declined even to tell your sheriff of the details. He was well vexed, I can tell you.'

'Yes, I think he mentioned something of the sort.'

'You have spoken to the sheriff about me? That won't answer.'

'It is rather the case that he spoke to me about you. He does not find you forthcoming and feels that you are holding back a good deal.'

'He got that right,' said Phelps. 'I cannot go running off at the mouth to all the world and his dog about this business. The ramifications are immense.'

Not for the first time, Bridges formed the impression that the policeman was trying to make himself sound more important than was in fact the case.

'What are these here ramifications of which you tell?' he asked.

The other man leaned forward in a conspiratorial manner. 'The head of the police in London, England has wrote to our department asking us to tackle this. He said that there was unease at the highest quarter, the *highest quarter* mark you, about this. My superior says the Queen herself has taken an interest in this affair.'

'That sounds like a pile of horse-crap to me,' declared Bridges. 'Why should the Queen of England set mind to what is going on at the Yellow Rose? It makes no sense. I think you are puffing yourself up.'

Phelps was outraged. 'Do you, hey?' he fumed, 'Well let me tell you, I have seen the letter that President Grant himself sent to our chief. He says that representations have been made to him by European heads of state. What do you say to that, hey?'

'I have discovered some few things over the last day or two, but I will not give you this information for free. I will trade you.'

'Trade me? Do you hear what you are saying? You purpose to obstruct an investigation ordered by the President himself. Think well what you are about.'

'I have thought long and hard on this,' said Bridges calmly. 'I don't think that the President enters into the case. You are just another private citizen in this town, same as me. What will you have? Do you want to share what we know together or would you rather that we both ploughed our own furrows? It is up to you.'

The policeman sat for a minute or so, considering this proposition. In the end, Bridges's mulish obstinacy defeated him, because he said, 'All right then. You go first.'

'That is just what I was going to say. Howsoever, I will oblige. Outside town, one of those who works for him you call the colonel had rented an old barn. He was storing bleach in it.'

'Bleach? What sort of bleach?'

'I cannot call to mind the name of it. It was not such as you would buy in a store, but was rather some chemical name.'

'Not sodium thiosulfate?'

'That's it. Your turn.'

'Quick man, tell me where this barn may be found. This is of the utmost importance.'

'Your turn,' said Bridges stolidly.

'Hell's afire, but you are the most stubborn man I ever did meet. All right, the colonel lives eight miles east of here on the road to St Louis. Now tell me where this store of sodium thiosulfate is to be found.'

Bridges told him and over the next five minutes, they pooled their information. The one thing that he held back was the location of the hidden rooms above the Yellow Rose. Phelps was evidently excited because he guessed that this mysterious room he was seeking might be found at the Richardson place. Bridges saw no reason to disabuse him of this belief. He had a personal grudge against Kirby and felt a proprietorial interest in the Yellow Rose. He wanted to tackle that part alone. Besides which, the one thing that the New York policeman still resolutely refused to reveal was the nature of the crime which he was investigating. So be it; if Phelps could play his cards close to his chest, so too could he.

After parting from Phelps, Bridges took a walk along Main Street to give himself a chance to set his thoughts in order. He fancied that people seemed a little less disposed to openly shun him as though he were an infected dog. He wondered if word might be getting round that he had had nothing to do with the murder of the girl. This set him thinking as to what efforts the sheriff was making in the direction of tracking down those who were really responsible for the crime, and so he headed over to the sheriff's office, where Mrs Larssen's nephew was just shutting up shop for the day.

'Oh, it's you Bridges,' was the unenthusiastic greeting he received.

'And a very good evening to you too, Sheriff,' he responded politely. 'I was just wondering if you are any forrarder in your investigation into young Ellie's death?'

'As I passed that eating house, did I catch a sight of you consulting with that man from New York?'

'It might be so. Why do you ask?'

'Because he is a damned nuisance. I have received a telegram from the state capital today, instructing me to 'render every practical assistance to this officer in his enquiries'. It is in my mind that he must have gone scuttling off and telling tales of me.'

'He is a close one. He will not say what he is on the track of, except where President Grant himself has a personal interest in the matter.'

'He told me the selfsame thing. I think it is a lot of shit, to speak plainly.'

'That was my thought, also.'

'You are, I notice, still in town, Bridges. Do you mind telling me what you are remaining here for?'

'I wonder you ask me. I wish to see the killers of that child brought to book and also have it in mind to settle scores with those who tried to pin that deed on me.'

'I have already warned you,' said the sheriff, 'about taking any action which might undermine my lawful authority or could look like a revenge killing. You have not forgot this?'

Bridges was all innocence as he answered, 'When I talk of settling scores, I mean only that I wish for them to answer in a court of law for what they done. Nothing more.'

'Did Phelps tell you anything useful?'

'Apart from how the Queen of England and the President of the USA are relying upon him? No, not really. He thinks that if he pulls off whatever this is, it will do him some personal good. That at least is my reading of the situation.'

* * *

After parting on fairly good terms from Sheriff Tucker who, he suspected, knew very well that he was proposing to go after Kirby, Bridges thought that it was time to be a little bold. He accordingly directed his way to the Yellow Rose to ask his former employer for the wages owed to him. He did not really need the money, as he had barely spent any of the money he had been paid after the last drive, but it was more that he was interested to see what Kirby would make of him just turning up at the Yellow Rose.

Kirby stared at his former help as though he were a ghost. 'I do not want any trouble here, you hear what I say? I don't know what you suspect of me, but I'll warrant it is not true.'

Bridges considered this statement carefully for a while. Then he said, 'You don't know what I think, but whatever it is is untrue. Is that how you see the case? That's a strange point of view. You mean if I thought that you were an honest and virtuous man who would not perjure himself to send a fellow being to the gallows, then I would be mistaken about that? I see.'

'What do you want, Bridges?'

'I want the wages you owe me. I also want to check round my room to make certain-sure that I have not left any of my belongings behind.'

'You sure you not fixing to cause trouble?'

'Trouble, Kirby? Why should you think that?'

'Wait here. I will get you your money and then take you upstairs to check the room. I hope we may part friends?'

'Do you?' said Bridges. 'Why ever should we not?'

As they reached the first-floor landing on the way up to the top of the building, Bridges cast a swift and surreptitious look at the corridor that branched off towards the back of the place. Just as he remembered, it stopped short after thirty feet or so, ending in a new and solid looking door. There was nothing of his in the room, but then he had already known that.

As they parted, Kirby offered his

hand to Bridges, saying, 'No hard feelings.'

Since this was a man whom Bridges was aiming to go after, it would have sat ill with him to shake hands and so indicate to the man that there was peace between them. Instead, he nodded his head and said, 'So long, Kirby.'

Bridges had the feeling that the time would not be long delayed until he met Kirby again and on that next occasion, there was apt to be a reckoning for both the death of Ellie Cartwright and also the shameful way that he had almost been railroaded into getting hanged. Before this time came, though, he wanted first to talk to Mrs Larssen and hear her views and opinions about one or two things.

The evening meal was about to be set on the table when he arrived. He had time to freshen himself up and then the two of them set down to eat. He had been planning to ask a few questions of the widow Larssen, but she forestalled him, saying,

'I mind that you are hell bent on vengeance for the way you were treated. I suppose that you are setting out on that road either this day or the next?'

It was not often that he was completely lost for words, but Bridges found himself sitting there with his mouth hanging open in a most uncouth manner.

He said, 'Has your nephew spoke of this?'

'My nephew? What has he to do with this? I have eyes in my head and have walked this earth for long enough to know when trouble is brewing.'

'I do not know,' said Bridges, 'as I should call this vengeance. There is the death of a young girl to answer for. You think that we should forget her so soon?'

'I said nothing of forgetting her,' she said sharply. 'But think on this. What would this country be like if every man were a law unto himself? That is why we have courts and judges, sheriffs and police, so that men do not just hunt down their enemies and slay them out of hand. Have you heard tell of a man called Thomas Hobbes?'

'I do not recollect the name.'

'He was an Englishman during their civil war, some hundreds of years since. He wrote of what things would be like if there was no society and everybody did as they pleased. As I recall, he said that in such a time, each man was 'constrained only by his imagination, ferocity and daring' and that the life of men would be 'nasty, brutish and short'. Good reason for leaving it to the law to settle disputes.'

Although he was not a one for deep thinking and knew little enough of political philosophy, still, Bridges thought that there was a flaw in this reasoning, if only he were able to put his finger on it. After considering, he said,

'Begging you pardon, ma'am, but that isn't quite the case, even when there are no judges and sheriffs close to hand.'

'Go on.'

'Have you ever heard of the rattle-snake code?'

'It rings a bell.'

'When there are no regular lawmen around, there are still rules and standards by which we live. Even the roughest of men will abide by that code. Nobody wrote it down and there are no courts to punish those who break it, but me and others have lived by that code our whole lives long.'

'Ha, you think that does instead of a regular law code?'

'Not exactly,' said Bridges slowly. 'But sometimes it does better. With the rattlesnake code, you know you must tell a man when you are at outs with him, so that he is on his guard. The law does not oblige me to do that. Today, a man wanted to shake my hand and I refused, because it would have lulled him into thinking that there was no enmity between us. I think that would be dishonourable, since I am fixing to go after him. It's nothing illegal, though, to shake hands and still plan evil.'

Mrs Larssen looked at Bridges for a long moment. Then she said,

'For a man who represents himself as a plain cowboy who is somewhat slow of speech, you are a right deep thinker, Mr Bridges. A right deep thinker.'

'I have never been called that before, ma'am,' said Bridges with a smile on his face.

'Just promise me one thing,' said Mrs Larssen. 'Promise me that before you take whatever action you have in mind, you will make sure to examine your heart and be sure of your true motive. Will you do that for me?'

'I will, ma'am. I promise you that.'

After they had finished eating and Bridges had helped wash up the wares, he went to his room and checked over his gear. He kept his saddle roll here and also his rifle. He had won the Winchester 73 in a poker game the previous year and was right proud of it. It was the hell of a gun if you wanted to fire off a lot of fast, accurate shots. And let's face it, what more could you ask from a weapon? He stripped and oiled both the rifle and his pistol, cleaning them carefully with fragments of lint and using a pull-through to make sure the barrel was in good shape as well. Then he loaded them both and propped the Winchester by the side of his bed. He took off his boots and stretched out for a nap. It was past seven and he did not purpose to undertake anything for at least three or four hours.

8

When Bridges woke up it was pitch dark outside and he judged by the moon shining through the window that it was around nine. He pulled on his boots and prepared for action.

His intention was in the first instance to investigate the room over the Yellow Rose and see what was going on there. Depending upon what he found, he would try to turn Kirby in to the law and then go and pay the 'colonel' a visit and see what he had to say for himself. He hoped too to come across the other man who had been detaining the dead girl.

Since he was reasonably sure that this man had also killed Ellie, he would not be over fussy about shooting this fellow if he fetched up against him.

Mrs Larssen was in the front parlour, the light turned low by her side, and she was reading the Bible. He paused at the door and coughed discreetly.

'I am going out for a spell, ma'am. I may not be back tonight, depending upon circumstances, as you could say.'

She closed the book and stood up. 'Well, Mr Bridges, you are set in your course, I can see that clear enough. I only hope that you will take care of yourself and set mind to what I told you earlier.'

'I hope that I shall be able to bring those men as killed that child to book. It is my aim to deliver them to your nephew if I am able. If not, well then I must see what chances. Goodnight, ma'am.'

'Goodnight to you, Mr Bridges. And good luck.'

★　★　★

Main Street was a bustling hive of activity. Another drive had hit town that day and the boys were eager to throw their money around. All the saloons were doing good business and the stores had remained open in case anybody was minded to spend their cash on such prosaic and down-to-earth items as razors, boots, rope or lamp oil.

Bridges went into the hardware store and asked to look at some spades. He cut a strange and somewhat forbidding figure if he did but know it. It was not common to see a man walk around town carrying a rifle under his arm. Not that there was any law against it and it was nothing to the clerk in the store.

'This here is a popular line,' said the clerk, showing Bridges a feeble-looking item which would like as not fall apart as soon as you thrust it into the ground.

'No,' said Bridges, 'I need something stronger than that. It also needs a narrower blade.'

The man produced a couple more spades from out the back, one of which was just exactly what Bridges wanted. He paid for it and then headed off to the back of the Yellow Rose.

Before breaking into the space over

the saloon, Bridges wanted to be quite sure that there was nobody there. He stashed the spade in the alleyway and then climbed on to the roof of the telegraph office, figuring that nobody was apt to see him at night. From this vantage point he could see lights shining through the skylights on the roof of the Yellow Rose. Then, as he watched, he saw something most surprising. There was a bright flash of light. He thought at first that it might have been the flash from a gun being discharged, but there was no sound of a shot. He stayed where he was, and a few minutes later there was another flash, which lit up the skylights from within.

'What the hell is going on in there?' he muttered to himself.

Bridges wanted to break into the Yellow Rose while it was busy and crowded. There is no worse time to break into somewhere than the middle of the night, when everybody is quiet and there is no noise. At such a time, even a creaking floorboard will cause sleepers to stir uneasily. When the Yellow Rose was going strong, you could set off a stick of dynamite and, like as not, nobody would hear it. Still, he did not wish to enter the upper storey while people were there. He would have to come back later.

Toting a Winchester round while killing time on a Friday night was not the smart dodge. It would alert all and sundry to the fact that he was most likely on the warpath. That being so, he left the gun on the roof, ready to retrieve later when he was ready for action. In the meantime, a shot of whiskey would do no harm.

The Golden Nugget was one of the smallest of the saloons in Stockton. Folk only really went there for one reason and that was the faro table. An awful lot of cash changed hands at the Golden Nugget and although Bridges was not a gambling man, he liked to watch the game with a drink in his hand.

The first person he saw when he entered the place was Phelps, the policeman from New York. Bridges nearly turned right around and walked out, but on reflection it could do no harm to see what the fellow was up to.

Once he had his whiskey Bridges wandered over to the table and stood next to Phelps.

'You betting or just watching?' he enquired.

'Hey there, Bridges,' said Phelps. 'A bit of both, I guess.' It was easy to work out from his flushed face and slightly slurred speech that Phelps was not a temperance man. 'Where have you been all evening? I had something to say to you.'

'Well,' said Bridges, 'I am here now.'

'It was this. You did not mention if you had run to earth the big room with plenty of light about which I was making enquiry. I went up to that barn you told me of, thinking that that might be the place, but it was nothing of the sort. I gather that the man who was staying in that barn with that stockpile of sodium thiosulfate is now deceased.'

'Yes, that is so.'

'Did you kill him?'

'No, but I wish that I had. It was the sheriff.'

'Was there anything of interest on his person?'

'If there was, then I have not heard about it.' said Bridges. 'Are you fixing to tell me what you are about here? By which I mean what sort of crime you are trying to act against? If you will, then I might be able to help you out.'

'Oh, you're a cunning one, Bridges,' said the policeman. 'All along, I think that you know where the place is that I am after and here you are foxing with me and trying to pump me. Yes, you are a cunning one all right.'

'Nothing of the sort,' said Bridges. 'I am only a cowboy. Well, will you tell me what you are about?'

'I will not. I am not having another man steal my glory on this case. That has happened before, you know. A fellow puts all his effort into an investigation and then some dirty scoundrel comes along and takes over the case. No sir, that is not happening to me again. I know what I know and you know what you know.'

'Just as you like.'

'You may hear something about this in the morning, Bridges. I purpose to take some startling action this very night.'

'I should keep your voice down about that, were I you. You have been drinking by the look of it. I would not go taking any rash actions in the state you are in.'

'You tend to your affairs and I shall do the same.'

Bridges shrugged. 'It's your funeral.'

After he had finished his drink, Bridges took a walk up and down the street. It was cheery to see all the lights blazing and people having a good, if noisy, time. He went past the Yellow Rose, to check whether it was busy and if there was a good lot of noise being generated there, which was certainly the case. Time to check again if the upstairs was still in use.

Back on the roof, Bridges was just in time to see the glow of an oil lamp fade and die beneath the skylights of the building opposite. This meant perhaps that whoever was in there was about to leave, and on an impulse he snatched up his rifle and hurried down the fire escape.

His guess was spot on, because as he stood in the shadow of the telegraph office he saw the back door of the Yellow Rose open and a figure emerge. Bridges shrank deeper into the shadows. There was the sharp click as the door was locked and then the man, for so it appeared: at any rate it was somebody wearing pants, walked towards him.

Just at that moment the moon came out from behind a cloud and the fellow's face was illuminated as though it were midday. It was the other one of the pair who had been in charge of Ellie Cartwright when he had first encountered her. Bridges stepped out of the shadows, right in front of the man.

'I've got a crow to pluck with you,' he said.

Some men in that situation would have prevaricated and played for time. Others would have been taken aback and begun to stutter or bluster. This man did none of those things. He just pulled out a gun from a concealed holster and shot Bridges at point-blank range.

Now by the purest chance the bullet, which was heading straight for Bridges's heart, instead struck the breech of the Winchester and was deflected. It went whining off into the night sky. Whereupon Bridges raised the rifle and cocked it in one smooth movement and then squeezed the trigger.

The man flinched as he heard the click, but nothing happened. It passed swiftly through Bridges's mind that the bullet's hitting the metal-work of the rifle must have done it a mischief.

Rather than drop it in order to go for his pistol, he swung the barrel into the man's face, cutting open his cheek. Then he brought it down hard on the wrist holding the gun which had been fired at him. There was a sickening crack as the bone snapped.

'I have been hoping to run into you,' said Bridges in a conversational tone, like he might be about to discuss the weather or something. 'I am minded to kill you for what you and your partner did to that girl.'

The man was bent over, his hand hanging useless and his pistol lying on the ground where he had dropped it.

'You broke my arm,' he said. 'What will become of me? It is my right hand.'

'If you live long enough it might heal,' said Bridges reassuringly. 'But truth to tell, I do not think that your life will be very long. Either I will shoot you down like a mad dog here and now or I shall hand you over to the sheriff and you will hang. In either event, I shouldn't worry none about your broken arm. It does not signify.'

'I didn't kill her, you bastard,' said the man. 'Me and my partner had no part in it. We just told a certain person where she was and that was the end of our interest. You have the wrong man.'

'Do you say that you didn't fetch her out of her home and then drug her?'

'That's nothing,' began the man and then screamed in agony when Bridges slammed the stock of his rifle down on the injured wrist.

'Nothing, is it?' he said. 'Nothing to take a poor, defenceless child from her mother for the Lord knows what purpose and then drug her? Nothing to be a part of some beastliness which ends in her death? Was that nothing?'

The man fell silent, gauging quite correctly that his life was hanging in the balance. One wrong word from him now would be enough to enrage Bridges to the point when he would pull out his pistol and just shoot him out of hand.

The two of them stood there for a

short while and then the moment passed. If Bridges had been going to kill him, it would have happened. They both knew that whatever else he did, he was not going to kill a wounded and helpless man.

Nobody could have heard the shot or, if they had, they were not inclined to investigate it. The man was nursing his wrist and blood was dripping from the gash across his cheek.

He said, 'You not only done in my arm, you damn near took out my eye.'

'Shut up,' said Bridges. 'You are lucky to be alive. You shot at me, if you recollect. You are lucky not to have got worse. Here is what we will do. I am not going to kill you, but will instead hand you over to the sheriff. I don't much care if you end up getting hanged. That is nothing to me.'

The wounded man said nothing. Secretly, he was feeling relieved to learn that this fellow was not planning to kill him on the spot.

'In return for this mercy,' continued

Bridges, 'I want something from you. I hear your precious boss lives out on the St Louis road. Is that so?'

'That is where the colonel lives, yes.'

'I wish to take some small action this night and also tomorrow morning. I want you to give the sheriff no information about either where he may find the colonel or about this place,' said Bridges, indicating the Yellow Rose with a wave of his hand. 'I dare say that you will be able to get your arm fixed up and suchlike. If you do not agree to this, I shall rough you up and make sure that wrist of yours is so broken up that it never heals. What do you say?'

The man shrugged. 'I do not think,' he observed, 'as I have much choice.'

After getting the man to describe in detail the route to and appearance of the farmhouse where the colonel was living, Bridges marched him along the street at gunpoint, which created some little interest from passers by. Some of them recognized Bridges as the man lately suspected of the murder of Ellie

Cartwright and they wondered what the game could be.

The sheriff's office was closed up, but an officious loafer informed Bridges that he could be found near to the Golden Eagle, where there had been a man knifed earlier that evening.

Furnishing this information to Bridges was not in the nature of a disinterested act on the part of the fellow. He was itching to find out what was going on and felt that this end could be best achieved by putting this man and his captive on the trail of the sheriff. He could then tag along and listen to what was said, so finding out what was what.

Tucker was not overjoyed to see Bridges. He was pleased enough to find that he had apprehended one of the people concerned in the death of Ellie Cartwright, but was irritated to find that the man had been badly injured during the process.

'Jesus, Bridges, did you have to hurt him this bad? He looks to me like he will need a doctor before the night is out.'

'What about the knifing you were said to be looking into,' said Bridges helpfully. 'Could you not send for the doctor and he could deal with both my man and the victim here at the same time?'

'You are getting a mite too smart for my taste, Bridges, you know that? In any case, there is no doctor needed here, but rather the undertaker.'

'Well, Sheriff, I have taken this man and now handed him over to you. As I see it, my part is done and I shall bid you goodnight.'

'Not so fast. You can come along to the office with me. I will need to write up something about this, giving your particulars.'

'Can it not wait? I would be heading to bed soon.'

'No it can't. Have you seen Phelps this evening?'

'Yes, he was in the Golden Eagle. Why do you ask?'

'I don't trust that fellow, for all that I have been told to help him. You still don't know what he is after?'

'No,' said Bridges. 'He is playing his cards right close to his chest.'

At this point the injured man interrupted, saying, 'The two of you are gossiping like old women while I am in pain. Not to mention where I am losing a lot of blood. I need a doctor.'

'Don't take that line,' said the sheriff coldly. 'If it is true that you had charge of that girl as died, then I tell you right now that you are a mangy cur and I will do my utmost to see you hanged.' Despite these harsh words, he consented to make off in the direction of his office.

As they walked there, the sheriff said to Bridges, 'My patience is about wore away with you now, you know. You have achieved what you wanted and found the men who you saw with the girl that night. One is dead and you have messed up the other to no small degree. I think your thirst for vengeance should now be satisfied.'

'I cannot be blamed for this night's happenings. I bumped into this man and he shot at me. How can you lay that at my door?'

'Yes,' said the sheriff. 'He shot at you, and by your own account the bullet ricocheted off your rifle there. Would you care to explain how it was you chanced to be roaming round town carrying a Winchester '73?'

Bridges remained silent and none of the three spoke again until the man with the broken wrist was safely locked up in the cell that Bridges had lately occupied in the back of the sheriff's office. Sheriff Tucker poked up the stove, managed to get a fire going and asked Bridges if he would care to stay while a pot of coffee was brewed, to which he received ready assent.

When the two men were settled down with their coffee, Tucker said, 'I cannot make you out, Bridges. You seem at first sight like somebody who is polite, quiet and a little . . . ' he struggled to find a word that would not be too insulting to the man sitting opposite him in the dimly lit office.

'Slow?' suggested Bridges, with a smile.

'If you like, yes. Yet here you are, racing round town wreaking vengeance on those who have wronged you. And the devil of it is, you never actually seem to do much. All the action looks to take you by surprise.'

There was a querulous shout from the cell. 'There's a man in here with a broke wrist, in case you had forgotten. Least you could do would be to fetch a doctor and maybe let me have a cup of that coffee.'

'Shut up!' shouted back the sheriff.

'I have took up enough of your time,' said Bridges. 'I must be going.' He stood up and moved towards the door.

'Not so fast. Do you plan to go bumping into any more trouble?'

'Not a bit of it,' said Bridges, evidently surprised by the question. 'I am going home to bed now.'

'Well then, goodnight to you.'

★ ★ ★

Having taken his leave of the sheriff, Chris Bridges went straight to the telegraph office. His purpose all along that night had been to break down the back door of the Yellow Rose and see what this precious secret was that was being hidden there; a secret which had led to Ellie Cartwright's death and brought him within a whisker of being hanged. He paused for a moment in the alleyway alongside the telegraph office. Then he went to retrieve his spade from where he had left it. Nothing like a stout spade for levering open a door.

Out of the corner of his eye he glimpsed movement and whirled round to find a man creeping up behind him. His gun was in his hand in a fraction of a second and he drew down on the fellow who was trying to take him by surprise.

'Come out now from those shadows,

or by God I will fire!'

The man stepped forward to where Bridges could see him clearly.

'Phelps!' cried Bridges. 'What are you doing slinking around here like an alley cat?'

'Knew you was up to something. I just knew it. Knew, knew, knew it. I did. I knew it.'

'You're drunk man. Get on out of here, I am busy.'

'I knew that if I just followed you, you would lead me somewhere. Been trailing you the livelong night. What do you say to that, hey?'

'What do I say?' asked Bridges. 'Why, I say that you are a drunken fool. Now just you run along out of here.'

Phelps was leaning against the wall, showing every sign of extreme intoxication. Reasoning with him would be hopeless and Bridges toyed briefly with the idea of fetching that spade and banging the man over the head with it to knock him out.

'Yes,' said Phelps, 'I knew it all right.

Everybody plays those sorts of tricks on me. Wait 'til a case is nearly solved and then cuts in on me and takes the glory. Well not this time, oh no. This time, Cornelius Phelps is going to be the hero.'

'There are no heroes,' said Bridges. 'I simply want to find out what has been going on. I am not aiming to take the credit for anything. I promise I will leave anything of that sort to you. Just leave me now and I will tell you all about it in the morning.'

'No sir, I ain't agoing anywhere, let me tell you. Nowhere at all. I am waiting right here to see what you are about.'

It would be madness to break into the Yellow Rose with this drunk in tow and Bridges reluctantly abandoned the idea; at least for that night.

'Listen, Phelps, I only stepped into this here alley to make water. I am going for to ride off now. My horse is at the livery stable down the road a pace. Why don't you go off now and sober up? We will talk more on this in the morning.'

Phelps was now slumped against the wall with his eyes closed. For a second, Bridges considered going ahead and busting down the door at the back of the Yellow Rose, but he could not be sure that Phelps would not wake up and begin shouting or otherwise causing a commotion. It was a damned nuisance, but he would have to give up the idea for now of solving this entire mystery tonight.

After helping Phelps to get back to the saloon where he was renting a room, with the man alternately cursing him and swearing undying friendship, to say nothing of sicking up on the side-walk, Bridges fetched his horse out of the livery stable. There was nobody around, but he figured that that did not signify, because it was after all his own horse and tack he was taking.

9

It was a fine, crisp night for riding. He had forgotten the pleasure of being out like this on horseback, with the noise and stink of the town far behind him. Bridges reined in the horse to revel in the sheer sensuous pleasure of being in open country, with nobody near to him and no racket from other folks and their affairs. It was like balm to his soul.

'I have surely missed this,' he said to himself. 'I cannot think what I was doing, planning to spend the winter holed up, being stuck cheek by jowl with a lot of people who never seem able to say straight what they mean.'

He rode on along the St Louis road at a leisurely trot, drinking in the smell of the earth and the glorious silence around him. This was the thing with towns and Bridges had found it before. Once you were in one, it kind of sucked you in and you found yourself getting caught up in a maelstrom. Never any time to stop and think about what you were doing, just buffeted from one encounter to the next.

That, at least, was how it had in the past appeared to him and his recent experiences had done nothing to dispel his prejudices against urban life.

He rode on for seven, maybe eight miles, until he came to one or two landmarks which had been given him by the man whose arm he had broken. He was tolerably sure now that he was within easy striking distance of the farmhouse where he might find the famous 'colonel' who seemed to be at the heart of all this. The man who, if his informant were to be believed, was ultimately responsible for the death of young Ellie and had encouraged Marion to try and get him to answer for the murder.

Bridges saw the farmhouse for which he was looking, nestled beneath a hill and half a mile off the road. There were lights on there, which presumably meant that people were at home; including, he supposed, the colonel. It was not his intention to brace them this night. A far better bet would be to wait until first light, when courage sleeps, even in the brave. He directed his horse at a walk towards a grove of trees which stood at the crown of the hill.

After having secured Jake to one of the trees, Bridges took a walk beyond the trees to savour the night sky. The band of the Milky Way straddled the sky and there was no sound at all, apart from the odd call of night birds or rustling from where some small animal was foraging.

He stood there, simply filled with pleasure and satisfaction at being away from that damned town and all its nonsense. It was a sharp night, but Bridges didn't care at all. The air was fragrant and clean and the world around him seemed a lot more real and important than the foolishness of the last few days.

As he lay down, resting his head on the saddle which he had removed from the horse, Bridges could not imagine what had been going through his mind to make him forswear the open air and decide rather to live in a dirty town. He surely could not have been thinking straight when he made such a decision.

Still, it was not too late to make the turnaround on that score and as soon as he had settled things here, he would have to be heading south again. He could not endure much more of this town life and that was a fact!

It felt so good to be sleeping out of doors again that Bridges forgot all the complaints that he had voiced about being cold, tired and worn out. The fresh air rather acted on him like a tonic and he had the best night's sleep since he had been living in the town. True, he had one or two minor aches and cramps, but they were nothing. He did not at all feel the muzzy-headedness that he had got used to when waking up in the morning after spending a night in a soft bed and the windows closed.

There was nothing to eat and so no point in fretting over breakfast. Maybe he would be able to get something after he had settled up with the men in that house. There was no sign of life from the place, no cock crowing or curling smoke from the chimney as somebody prepared breakfast. Mind, it was early yet: barely dawn.

Bridges checked his pistol, spinning the barrel and cocking the piece a couple of times to make sure that there was no stiffness in the mechanism. After he had done this, he had a good look at the Winchester. The bullet had buckled the plate, right where the hammer fell. It could be fixed, but he would need a vice and other tools to do it. He would have to rely only upon the handgun this day at least. Upon which reflection he patted the horse and set off down the hill to the farmhouse.

Once he reached the picket fence surrounding the house Bridges drew his pistol and cocked it. Then he opened the neatly painted white gate and walked across the yard to the front door. To his surprise, it was unlocked and unbolted.

He entered the house and then stopped for a few seconds to listen. There was no sound, other than that of a longcase clock near the stairs. Standing there, hardly even breathing, Bridges was pretty sure that there was nobody downstairs in the house. He still thought it prudent to check every room.

The house gave one the distinct impression of being used by a bunch of men with no moderating or refining female influence at all. A fruit bowl had been dragooned into service as a makeshift ashtray, presumably because it would need to be emptied less frequently. Even so, there were also cigar butts on the floor, along with brownish tobacco stains.

At a guess, those occupying the house thought nothing of expectorating wherever they felt the need. Dirty glasses crowded every available surface and jostled for space with empty whiskey bottles. Bridges himself had spent years living in bunkhouses and was no stranger to dirt and masculine disorder; never, though, had he seen this level of squalor.

Everywhere he looked there was fresh evidence of rough men who didn't care a fig how they left a place. From the rank atmosphere it was obvious to Bridges that nobody had opened a window to air any of the rooms in a good long while. In one corner of the biggest room were half a dozen military rifles.

Having assured himself that nobody down here was about to jump out and surprise him by taking a shot at him, as had happened not twelve hours since, it was time to look at the upper storey.

Before doing this though, he quietly bolted both front and back door from the inside. He did not want to worry about anybody entering the house and then coming up behind him. No point in being caught between the hammer and the anvil, as his grandma would have put it.

The stairs were carpeted and Bridges wondered about this house he was in. Had these men bought it? Were they just using it, or what? Surely, nobody who owned a house like this would treat it so. As he neared the top of the stairs Bridges took up first pull on the trigger. It would only take the least pressure now for him to fire.

The first room in which he looked was empty and it seemed like somebody had been sleeping on the floor. A blanket and saddle roll were there, with various personal belongings scattered around. The door to another room was open and he looked in, seeing a large bed with a man asleep in it. A quick check of the other rooms showed that there was only this one person in the whole, entire house.

'Wake up!' called Bridges roughly from the doorway. 'Come on, you lazy son of a bitch, the day is half-done. Rise and shine.'

The man in the bed stirred and then sat up. He was wearing a nightshirt and had on his head a ridiculous nightcap. It was the man whom he had thrown out of the musical theatre after he had seen him run his hands over Marion.

'Well, ain't you the dandy,' said Bridges mockingly. 'I mind that I know you. Happen you are the one they call the colonel?'

The man stretched his arms as though he had had a good night's sleep. Then he reached back towards his pillow.

'Do not move that hand, mister,' said Bridges, 'I will take oath that you have a pistol under that pillow and if you go for it, you are a dead man.'

'Colonel,' said the man. 'Not 'mister' but 'colonel'. Colonel Fraser. It is a small matter, but one of great importance to me. How did you find me?'

'Don't you set mind to that,' said Bridges. 'Just get yourself dressed.'

'With an audience?' asked the man, apparently shocked at the idea. 'Surely you cannot be serious?'

'Just don't follow any instruction which I give you and you will soon find out how serious I am. I tell you now, before God, I am more than half minded to shoot you down now. It would not take much to make up my mind and do it. Do not put it to the test.'

'Just as you will. You appear from where I am sitting to be holding all the cards.'

'You got that right.'

Colonel Fraser got out of bed and took off his nightgown. He did not appear to mind particularly about being seen without any clothing. When he was fully dressed, in an elegant and expensive but not ostentatious style, he stood in front of Bridges and said,

'What now? You are of course the unfortunate fellow whom we wished to answer for that stupid child's death.'

'Don't say nothing nasty about her,

Fraser, or I'm like to shoot you where you stand.'

Fraser smiled at him. 'Only you won't, will you? I know your type; you would not dream of killing an unarmed man. If I tried to walk out of here now, you would feel it right and justifiable to stop me by using your fists, but never in a thousand years would you gun me down without I had a weapon of my own. You're one of those 'rattlesnake code' boys. I know your sort.'

'Would you care to put that to the test this minute?'

'To speak plainly, no I would not. What will you do now? Take me into town to the sheriff?'

'No,' said Bridges, 'This is between the two of us. The sheriff does not enter into the reckoning.'

'Well, what then? May we have breakfast while you tell me?'

'No, I will not sit at table with a man I propose to kill. It would not set well with me. We will deal with this now and then, if either of us is alive afterwards, there will be time then for eating. Did you kill Ellie Cartwright?'

'She was no further use to me. Also, since you had her, there was the possibility that she could cause me embarrasment.'

'And I suppose it was your plan to fix the crime on me and see me hang for it?'

'Of course. Nobody would have missed you. You are a no-count cowboy.'

'One last thing, are you really a colonel? I guess from how you speak that you are from Virginia?'

'Not a bad guess. North Carolina. Yes, I was a colonel in the Confederate army. You know, I have enjoyed visiting with you, but this really isn't business. I am hungry and there are things I should be seeing to. If there is nothing else . . . ?' Colonel Fraser waved his hand languidly, as though dismissing a waiter or barkeep.

'You have a pistol and holster round here, I'll be bound,' said Bridges.

'Yes, over there on the table. Surely you are not going to propose a quick-draw gunfight? You will lose.'

'It could be so, but why would you be worried?' said the imperturbable cowboy. 'Just back away there, where I can keep an eye on you and you are not tempted to go for that piece you keep under your pillow.'

The colonel's pistol was an old-fashioned one: a single action cap-and-ball revolver. It was Colt's 1860 army model. The steel was blued, giving the piece a beautiful look. Bridges hefted it in his hand. 'Did you carry this in the war?'

'Yes, that's right. From your own voice, I would judge that we were on the same side. Does that mean anything at all to you?'

'No,' said Bridges. 'Not a damned thing.'

'No, nor to me,' said Fraser. 'Well, what do you want to do next?'

'We will go down the stairs slowly and with you in front of me. I will bring your rig along of me.'

When the two of them were standing at the foot of the stairs, Bridges still covering the other and not trusting him for a second, the ticking of the long-case was loud and clear.

'Is this a chiming clock?' asked Bridges.

'That's a queer thing to ask at a time like this,' said the colonel. 'Yes, it has a good, loud chime.'

'I suppose it is true what I was told, that you run a few girls in town who work as whores?'

'It's true enough. I don't wish to hurry you, but I have something I need to be about. The sooner I kill you, the sooner I can saddle up and ride off to deal with it. I don't wish to appear impatient or discourteous, you understand.'

'You are a cool customer,' said Bridges, with a hint of reluctant admiration in his voice. 'One more question. You know why I wish to kill you?'

'Of course,' said Fraser, surprised. 'I do not blame you in the least. I killed a little girl whom you had sworn to protect, from what I have since heard, and then I tried to get you hanged for it. It is only in reason that you should wish to settle with me over the matter.'

'How far do you suppose it is from that front door there to the kitchen back there?' asked Bridges.

'I should say some thirty feet. What have you in mind?'

'I suggest this. I will adjust the hands of that clock until they show a minute or two to the hour. We shall then take up our stand, one at this door and the other in the doorway to the kitchen. Then we will draw when the clock strikes. And I tell you now, you had best have made your peace with the Lord when that happens, because you will be dead before the striking ends.'

Colonel Fraser was pleased at the arrangement. It suited his humour to be a part of such a theatrical set-up, even if it meant that he would be in hazard of his life.

'Don't worry about the state of my soul, Bridges. I am not about to die. It would be better for you if you were to say a prayer.'

'One last thing troubles me,' said Bridges. 'It is this. Whoever stands by this door will have an advantage over the one who stands in the kitchen doorway. In the one case, the man in the doorway will be an outline against that window in the kitchen. The man by the door there will be in the shadows and will so have a double advantage. I will spin a coin and you call. The winner chooses his place to stand.'

'What a delicate conscience you have,' said Colonel Fraser. 'You are hell bent on killing me, but do not want to cheat. I never heard the like. Go on then and I will call.'

Bridges uncocked his piece and tucked it in his pants. Then he found a dime and spun it in the air.

'Heads!' called the colonel, and sure

enough, heads it was. 'I don't have your scruples, my friend,' he said. 'I shall stand here and you can be silhouetted against the light. I am determined not to be killed, you see.'

'Be determined as you like,' muttered Bridges.

Keeping a wary eye on the other, he opened the little window giving access to the hands of the clock and pushed the minute hand forward until it showed five minutes to seven. Then he carefully closed and fastened the window.

'I will hand you your rig,' said Bridges, 'and then back off to take my place in that doorway. I will be keeping you covered though, until you are ready, and I shall then replace my gun in its holster and we will wait for the chimes.'

As the colonel buckled on his gunbelt, Bridges backed slowly towards the kitchen, his gun cocked and ready in his hand, all the time watching Fraser to see if he was going to make his move before they were both ready. He needn't have worried. The former officer apparently had a sense of honour about matters of this sort. He had a sardonic look upon his face as he adjusted the holster and belt to his liking, the hilt of the pistol being precisely midway between his elbow and wrist.

Bridges uncocked his pistol, squeezing the trigger and lowering the hammer gently with his thumb. Then he put it in his holster and stood facing his opponent.

The two men stood in this way, facing each other like there was nothing much going on. Had you not seen the preparations, you would hardly have known that anything out of the ordinary was taking place. The tick of the clock was the only sound to be heard in the whole of the house. It was not a time for talking.

Despite their brave façades and earlier bantering words, no man squares up to death without some inward contemplation of his own mortality. Each earnestly believed that he would be the one to walk out of that house, leaving the dead body of his adversary. This did not prevent the gnawing worm of doubt to eat away at their vitals. No man is ever really confident of victory under such circumstances, no matter how boastful or outwardly calm.

Bridges was beginning to wonder if he had pushed the minute hand to five to the hour or maybe more like ten. Surely more than five minutes had elapsed since he had been fooling around with that little window? He tried to still his mind, empty it of all distractions. The only thing in the whole world that mattered in the next few seconds was being the first to get that pistol from the holster, cock it and kill the man in front of him.

This was not one of those times when a flesh wound would do the business; his first bullet would have to stop Fraser's heart, or sure as God made little apples, they would be carrying

Chris Bridges out of that house feet first in a pine casket. And still the longcase clock in the hallway sent out its monotonous rhythm of steady and measured ticks.

His grandma had had just such a clock in her house and Bridges recalled that, just before the chimc began at the hour, there was an almost imperceptible whirring as the mechanism geared up to strike the bell. He heard that faint sound now, just as he had when he was visting his grandma's house as a kid.

It was that ancient, long-forgotten memory that gave him the victory that day, because his hand began going for the gun just the tiniest fraction of a second before the clock chimed. Not long enough to compromise his honour or cause him later to accuse himself of cheating, but just enough in advance of the colonel to give him a razor thin advantage over the other man.

His hand reached the gun as the first chime sounded and was out of the holster before it had finished. He cocked it with his thumb as he drew and then fired almost instinctively towards the man in the darkened hallway.

The colonel's gun was in his hand, cocked and almost levelled at Chris Bridges when the bullet took him in his chest. He squeezed the trigger automatically, but had had no chance to aim. His shot went wild, slamming into the clock for whose chime they had been waiting. Bridges's next shot hit him just above the bridge of his nose, right between his eyes. He fell dead before having a chance to cock his piece a second time.

Bridges stood there, almost unable to believe that he was alive. The house was utterly silent after the crash of the gunfire. Even though his ears were ringing with the noise of the shooting in that confined space, it seemed to him that the silence had a quality which it had not had before the duel. It took him a second or two to work out what was different. Then it struck him. The clock was no longer ticking. Fraser's shot must have hit it and done some mischief to the works.

However bad a man has been in life, there is a certain feeling of reverence and awe at his passing. Even after the hanging of the worst villain, folk will hush their voices and behave with a little more decorum. He might not have had any respect for Colonel Fraser in life, but he deserved some small courtesy in death.

Going over to the corpse, Bridges looked at the dead man and said out loud,

'Well you were a bad man, which there is no denying, but you died like a man. I hope I gave you a better death than you would have had kicking out your last seconds at the end of a hang-rope. I hope you rest well.' Then he unbolted the door, stepped over the corpse and walked out into the morning sunshine.

As he walked up the hill to his horse, Bridges reflected on the strange fact that his grandma's having a certain kind of clock in her house had made the difference between life and death for him that day. It truly was the case; just that slight metallic hum before the hammer hit the bell, that had been all the edge he had against the colonel. Mind, he was quick enough on the draw, he always had been, but without that slightest of advantages he would never have beaten the other man.

He shivered suddenly: the feeling that folk sometimes call somebody walking over your grave. It had been a damned close thing and he knew that he was lucky still to be alive.

10

Bridges did not hurry back to town. It was a glorious morning and never had life seemed sweeter to him. All around him he could see living things. Trees, grass, birds overhead, the occasional jackrabbit hopping out of his path. He too was alive and he wished to savour the feeling, the knowledge that he had not died earlier that day, as he so very easily could have done.

There remained only one piece of unfinished business now and that was to find out what this had all been for. A young girl strangled and two men shot dead; another in jail and likely to hang. What could possibly be worth all this?

Then again, he thought, it need not be any great matter at all. The fact that this affair had cost the lives of three people did not necessarily mean that this was anything special. He had known quarrels and vendettas that erupted over some trifling cause and cost more than one life before they settled.

Men are like that sometimes. They will fight to the death over some half-heard word in a bar or because they feel that somebody has looked longingly at their wife or for any one of a thousand other reasons. The three deaths in this case might not have any great cause, no matter what Phelps was claiming.

When Stockton came into sight Bridges reined in and contemplated the town for a space. The pleasure that he had been experiencing during his ride this morning was starting to evaporate, like the morning dew on the grass, at the sight of all those houses and other buildings. He just did not rate living so.

When once he had got to the bottom of this little riddle he would be taking off, probably back to Texas. The night sleeping out in the open had invigorated him and he had missed the feel of a horse between his legs as well. These were simple joys, but the town had nothing to match them. What fool would rather sit playing cards in a smoky saloon, sooner than ride out on a day such as this in God's open air?

It was still early when he rode up Main Street. The storekeepers were opening up and people were gearing up for the day. He attracted no attention from anybody as he went to the livery stable to leave his horse there once more. He asked the fellow if it would be all right to prop his rifle up in the corner for the day and there was no objection. He did not look to be doing any more shooting after the affair with the colonel, but still and all there was no point in being encumbered by a useless firearm.

Before he did anything else, Bridges was starving hungry. He had not eaten a bite since the meal at Mrs Larssen's the night before. The eating-house was open for business and he ordered eggs and toast with a pot of black coffee.

After he had dealt with this, he felt somewhat more able to tackle the day ahead. While he was finishing up the last of the coffee, who should walk through the door but Phelps, who was, by the look of him, keen to speak to him.

After the man had ordered coffee and sat down opposite Bridges he began to speak in an angry and animated way.

'You are a regular pain in an unmentionable part of the body, you know that? What do you mean by taking into custody that man I was trailing? It has made my job ten times harder. Are you trying to make a name for yourself at my expense?'

While the policeman berated him angrily, Bridges sized him up. He looked to be in a pitiable condition. His face was chalk white and his eyes bloodshot. He had not shaved and looked a little down at heel. When the other man stopped talking to take breath, Bridges cut in and said:

'You are complaining like an old

woman. It does you no credit. If you hadn't have been drunk last night, maybe you would have had better hunting.'

This provoked a furious response from the other. 'Drunk was I? Drunk? Let me tell you how things stand. We of the detective branch have to mix with various low types and move in some bad company. It would stand out by a mile if I were to drink soda while all those around me were supping whiskey. Drunk!'

'Like I say,' continued Bridges, 'you was drunk last night and so fit for nothing. The man you spoke of tried to kill me. I hurt him, as you might have heard and he is like to hang. I have some better news for you, though, if you will sit still a minute and stop talking like a woman.'

'What then?'

'I do not think that that fellow I took last night is going to be in a special hurry to provide information to the sheriff. Every word he speaks is likely to put his head further in the noose, as you might say. Besides which, I requested him to remain silent for a time about one or two things. I will tell you all that I know.'

Bridges felt a little sorry for the New York policeman, who, truth to tell, did not seem to be all that good at his job. If he could do the man a favour, then he would. His own vengeance had been accomplished and all that now remained was some slight curiosity about what the whole thing had concerned. He was about to slake that curiosity in a short while and there was no reason why he should not cut the policeman in on this.

'Do you mean this?' asked Phelps. 'If so, then you are the first person for a good long while who has offered to help me in this case. Nobody will tell me a thing.'

'Nobody was minded to tell me anything neither,' observed Bridges, 'I have still found out all that was needful.'

'All?' said Phelps, with a stirring of hope. 'You mean to say that you have tracked down the space which I was looking for? Where is it then?'

'All in good time. Finish your coffee. We need first to check that there is nobody there. Mind, two of those involved are dead and one is now in jail, so I don't look to find it tenanted.'

'You are leaving the colonel out of your reckoning, my friend. He is a force to be taken into account, believe me.'

'Not any more.' said Bridges quietly.

'What can you mean by that?'

'Only that he is no longer anybody to set mind to, never mind be afeared of.'

'Why?' said Phelps. 'What has become of him?'

'He is dead.'

'Dead?' exclaimed Phelps in dismay. 'Dead? Are you sure? This is terrible news. I wanted that man alive. He was the key to it all. I will never be able to end this case in a satisfactory fashion now.' He brooded for a few moments, before saying with a sudden hope, 'Are you sure he is dead? How do you know this?'

'That don't signify. I can tell you though for certain sure that the man, Colonel Fraser, although you did not see fit to tell me his name, is now dead. He died suddenly this very morning.'

'How do you know about all this? I should have been told.'

'Listen, Phelps,' said Bridges kindly. 'I do not think much of your skills as a policeman, but I think we can do each other a bit of good here. Let's make medicine.'

'What then do you suggest?' asked Phelps suspiciously.

'Only this: that I help you to clear up this whole case of yours and that you take all credit for it, leaving me altogether out of the business, both now and later.'

The wily policeman could not grasp the concept of a man doing something for somebody else and not expecting a return on it.

'You mean you will not go chasing

after reward money or want to see yourself in the newspapers or aught of that sort?'

'God forbid!' said Bridges piously. 'I can think of nothing worse. All I ask is that at the end of it, when I have set you on the right track and given you all that you require, then you give me a plain account of the affair from start to end. I want only to know what I stumbled into unawares.'

'Well, we are not there yet,' said Phelps, 'unless you really know where the base of their operations is to be found.'

'I shall lead you there directly. It is only ten minutes from where we are sat.'

'And what about the colonel? How did he die and where may I find his corpse?'

'It was not in reason that a man of that stamp should live a long, healthy and prosperous life,' said Bridges. 'At least, not in the long run. He lies dead now at that farmhouse up on the St

Louis road. He is shot through the heart and the head. His own shot broke the longcase clock in the hallway. There, are you satisfied?'

'You give me your word on this?'

'If you like. Come now and we will see if we can finish this off.'

Phelps and Bridges walked around the Yellow Rose, which was all shut up. Bridges tried the door, banged on it a few times and hollered for Kirby. There was no response.

'I reckon he is out. He does not live on the premises and it is a mite early for him to have got here yet. Still, we had best not tarry.'

He led the other man round to the back of the saloon, where to his surprise, the spade that he had purchased was still leaning against the wall.

'You are not averse to a little breaking and entering, I suppose?' asked Bridges.

'It would not do for a man in my position to be mixed up in such things,' said Phelps primly. 'You do what is needful, while I wait round the corner here. Then, when you have effected access, I will come along and I have had no part in it.'

'Strikes me,' said Bridges, 'that you have too delicate a way with you to make a good policeman. If I had thought, I would have searched Fraser's body. I'll warrant he had the key to this door somewhere on his person.'

'Search his body? Was it you then that killed him?'

Bridges looked at him in amazement. 'I would have thought that that went without saying.'

Now a strong spade might be the best implement in the world for forcing open a locked door, but it makes more noise about the process than is comfortable if you are trying to keep the thing private. Bridges inserted the blade of the spade into the space between the frame and the door, right above a hinge. He leaned on it to force it in and then wiggled it about a bit to gain purchase. Whereupon he used it as a crowbar or lever.

There was a fearful noise of splintering wood and sharp grating of metal on metal. The first attempts did not take the door off its hinges, but opened the way to his second and third efforts, which were finally crowned with success.

After his first go Phelps's voice came to him from round the corner. 'God almighty man, you are making enough noise about it. Can you not be a little quieter?'

'You want to try?' asked Bridges, to which there was no reply.

Eventually, the door yielded. He had made such a racket getting it off its hinges that Bridges was seriously concerned that somebody would by now have gone to fetch the sheriff.

'Come out of hiding, Phelps,' he said. 'The job is done and all that now remains is for us to see what is up there.'

Just as he had suspected, Bridges found that the doorway led to a staircase leading to the upper storeys of the Yellow Rose. He guessed that a false wall separated this from the kitchen at back of the saloon. There was no light and so the two men walked slowly and cautiously upwards. There was a second door at the top of the staircase, but mercifully this was not locked. It opened to reveal an enormous room, covering about half the size of the bar-room below. It was brighter than any indoor space that Bridges had ever seen, because the ceiling was covered with skylights. The whole place was full of various equipment which took him a while to make sense of.

One wall of the large room was set up like the stage in a theatre. There was a raised platform with a painted backdrop depicting palm trees and pyramids. There was also a fake palm tree mocked up out of plaster of Paris, wood and paper. To one side of this stood a clay jar. In front of this odd tableau stood a large wooden box, mounted on a tripod. It was, Bridges supposed, a camera, but there were two lenses at the front, rather than just one. All round the room were laid costumes and what looked to him like theatrical props: swords, chains, whips and various other items. A black curtain concealed a large area at the back of the room.

Bridges could make nothing at all of the thing. He vaguely assumed that this must be either a private theatre or a photographic studio. But why anybody would kill to protect such an establishment, to say nothing of going to enormous efforts to keep it a secret, he could not imagine.

Phelps, who seemed overjoyed at what he saw, laughed at Bridges's bewilderment. 'Can't make it all out, hey?' he enquired jovially. 'Come over here and I will discover to you the nature of this enterprise. Pull up a chair, it is by way of being a long story. Also, you might like to cast your eyes over what is on this here table, which will also make the case more open to you.'

'You are full of yourself now, Phelps,' said Bridges a little sourly. 'Very full of yourself for a man who had made no headway at all in his investigations and just waited for others to unravel the puzzle for you. Do not go getting a swelled head, now.'

'Oh hush, man. You would be pleased too if you knew what this meant. It will be the making of me. I will be the most looked-up to man in the whole of the detective branch after this. Come and sit down and I shall explain.'

They sat opposite each other at a table piled with photographs and a curious contraption made of metal and wood, which had at the front what looked like a pair of eyeglasses. Bridges picked up one of the pictures idly. It was of two apparently identical photographs, printed side by side on a piece of pasteboard perhaps six inches long. He looked at the picture and then recoiled in horror. It showed a half-naked woman pleasuring a sheep. 'What the hell is that filth?' he asked.

Phelps chuckled. 'I did not have you pegged for a prude, Bridges. Never seen dirty pictures before?'

'Nothing like to that one.'

'Listen then, and I shall tell you the story. Have you heard tell of stereoscopes?'

'Not that I recall.'

'They are a big thing in England and some other European countries. You have a device like this here, and you put in a pair of photographs. I had best choose something which will not shock you too badly. This might do. It is a coloured one as well. Look here through these lenses now.'

Phelps handed him the strange gadget that had been lying on the table. Bridges looked through the glasses at the front and his jaw nearly dropped. Two naked women were embracing. They appeared to be in a forest and were tricked out to look like something from a fairy story. There were two astonishing things about this scene. The first was that they appeared as real and solid as the room about him. He felt like he could reach out and touch them. The other thing was that they were not black and white, like regular photographs, but coloured quite naturally. They looked utterly real. He continued to stare entranced at the vision.

'They're something else again, ain't they,' said Phelps proudly, as though he had had a hand in the process. 'The colours are good. I heard where the colonel had some Chink girls tinting them by hand. They look almost real, don't they?'

'How come they look solid?' asked Bridges.

''Cause they take two pictures side by side at the same time, just like your eyes see two images and combine them. Look at that camera. See how it has two lenses?'

'How does this tie in with all that has happened?'

'I will explain. These stereoscopes, as

they are called, are a big thing in England. Company there sold a half-million of them in the last few years. Folk buy the cards for them, which are mainly views of far-off places such as they would never be able to visit. China, India and suchlike.

'Now this is all well and good and believe it or not, the Queen of England herself got keen on the idea. They had a big exhibition there some years before the war and she was right taken with stereoscopic views. She even engaged to have her own family photographed so.'

'You are one long-winded fellow,' said Bridges. 'Where does this town fit into the picture?'

'You must know,' said Phelps, like he was delivering a lecture up on a stage, 'that well-off people have always enjoyed what you would term dirty pictures. Howsoever, these have been expensive, needing as they do an artist to paint a scene such as might excite one. You follow me? Lately, there have been what you call etchings. These are copies of such dirty paintings and are a sight cheaper than having to pay a man to paint a picture just for you.'

Bridges picked up another of the cards and inserted it into the viewer. This one showed what looked to his eye like a girl too young to be mixed up in such goings on, cowering before a man with his britches open at the front, like he was about to perform.

He shook his head in disgust. 'Some of these pictures are just terrible, Phelps. What say we take them outside and build a bonfire of them?'

'Burn them? You must be insane! Anyways, to continue the tale, the colonel's genius was to set to and produce pictures better than any oil painting and make them cheap enough so that anybody could afford them. He has been selling this stuff, the proper name for which is porn-og-raphy, if you was wanting to know, not only in the USA but also exporting it to Europe. That is where the trouble started.'

'How's that?'

'You recall that I told you that Queen Victoria was a fan of these here stereoscopic pictures? She has a big, big collection and is aways buying new ones. She sent off to some company in London and they sent her a batch which was supposed to show various scenes of life in this country. By which I mean Red Indians, wagons, waterfalls and all the rest of it.

'Now the thing is, the company which she ordered these from had been buying some of this stuff from the colonel, there being a lively market for it and it bringing in more cash than pictures of the Niagara Falls. Would you believe it, but one of these here types of picture got mixed in with the others that they sent her?'

'I am beginning to get the general idea. And she was displeased with what she saw, I take it?'

'Displeased is, as you might say, understating the case somewhat. I heard from my boss where she is shortsighted and put in one of these cards, thinking to see a harmless scene of redskin girls carrying water or some such, and lo and behold, it is a girl going down on a dog!'

Appalled as he was at the nature of the material in the studio, Bridges could not restrain a chuckle. 'I am guessing that after that, the fat was well and truly in the fire?'

'You got that right,' said Phelps. 'To cut a long story short, she sent for her secretary of the interior or whatever they call him there, asked him what the Sam Hill he meant by allowing such things to enter her country and be bought and sold. You know those types. It is one thing for rich people to enjoy their dirty pictures or porn-og-raphy, but it is a different thing entirely if ordinary folks acquires the habit. No telling where it will lead.' Phelps winked at the man facing him.

'I suppose that the English police got in touch with Washington or something?' hazarded Bridges.

'Well first, their police raided the man who had accidently sent the picture to the Queen. Then they found that there was more of this stuff circulating than anybody had guessed. They discovered where it was coming from and, if you will believe it, their Prime Minister was so worked up about it that he sent a message to President Grant. Yes, I'll wager that you thought I was making it up about the President, didn't you?'

'The thought crossed my mind,' admitted Bridges.

'Not a bit of it. You know that the English were more on the side of the Confederacy in the war? Well since it ended, Grant has been hell-bent on making our two countries friends. The English Prime Minister, he gave it out that this sort of thing was not helping relations between our countries and he would be obliged to the President if he would put a stop to it. Most was being shipped through New York, which is how I become involved.'

'Where did the bleach enter into the picture?'

'What bleach?' asked Phelps, with a look of incomprehension on his face.

'The bleach that I found in the Richardson barn.'

'You mean the sodium thiosulfate? That's what they call hypo or fixer. These boys did all their developing and you need a lot of that stuff.'

'Where did that poor child who was killed fit in to the case?'

'What you have seen here is nothing. Some men, they like to see girls who are, shall we say, a little young. They took pictures of young women who were not very well developed to cater for that market. By what I heard, that girl that was strangled looked a deal younger than her years.'

'That,' said Bridges, 'is one of the worst things I ever heard tell of in my life. I am not sorry now that I shot the man behind this racket.'

'Mind, most of them as was photographed were being paid well for it. The colonel ran a string of whores on the side, as you might know. These were brought up here to have their pictures taken.'

'I saw some strange flashes of light through the roof the other night. What might they have been?'

'Magnesium flares. They need a lot of daylight in general, but sometimes, for special effect, they use magnesium powder to brighten the scene.'

'Let's have silence for a space now, Phelps. I want to think this through.'

The policeman did not seem at all put out to be spoken to in this way. He busied himself around the studio, gathering evidence and organizing the photographs and viewers into neat piles. It was while he was engaged in this activity that the other door to the studio opened. Bridges had forgotten that access to the place could also be gained through the Yellow Rose itself. There was a sharp metallic click and Kirby entered the room on some errand or other.

Kirby could not at first take in what he was seeing. He was used to coming into the room and finding various people there, taking photographs and so on, but when he recognized Bridges he let out an oath and turned to flee. The other two were so surprised at this development that they neither of them went for their guns.

As he reached the door Kirby turned and, perhaps with the intention of discouraging pursuit, drew a pistol and fired back into the room. Bridges fired back, but his bullet hit the doorframe as Kirby ran off.

Bridges jumped up and cried to Phelps, 'Come on man, now is your chance for some glory. You may catch at least one of those scoundrels.'

The other man made no reply and did not move. Bridges looked down at him, suspecting that he was not over eager to risk his own life. Phelps was sitting there, with his hand on his chest.

Bridges squatted beside the man and

moved his hand gently from the wound. Phelps said nothing, he was breathing torturously and seemed to be trying to speak.

'Just sit still, there,' said Bridges, meaninglessly. As he watched, the man stopped breathing and died where he was sitting.

From somewhere outside came the sound of gunfire; a single shot at first, which was followed by a perfect fusillade of firing. I guess, thought Bridges to himself, that that is the end of Kirby and there is no point in me chasing him.

It turned out that Bridges's guess had been right, because shortly afterwards the sheriff entered the studio, accompanied by one of his deputies.

He said, 'I might have guessed that you would be here, Bridges. Every which way I turn, I seem to stumble across you.'

'He don't look in too good a state,' said the deputy, indicating the New York policeman.

'Neither would you under the circumstances,' said Bridges. 'He died not long since.'

'You know,' said the sheriff, 'I sometimes wondered what Kirby was up to here. Last year, he said that he was turning the Yellow Rose into a regular hotel. There were builders up here and there was banging and stuff being brought in and out. Then it all stopped and he gave it out that he had run out of money before the work had been finished. Said that it was all broke up and dangerous to go in. Nobody thought nothing of it. After all, it was his saloon and if he wanted to half-wreck it, that was his own affair. So this is what he was up to all along.'

'What befell Kirby, just now?' asked Bridges.

'Came running out of the front door of the saloon with a gun in his hand,' said Tucker. 'We were passing and called on him to stop, whereupon he shot at us. He is dead. What has been going on here?'

226

Without going into any detail, Bridges told the sheriff what Phelps had said.

The sheriff said, 'Yes, I understood from the telegram I received that it was an important business. It will do me no harm to have cracked this case.' He looked at Bridges. 'Of course I will give you due credit for your part in it all.'

'I don't want any of it,' said Bridges emphatically, his mouth twisted as though he had bitten on to something that tasted bad. 'Do that and then all those people who were lately wishing to lynch me will come fawning round and telling me what a fine fellow I am? No thank you. You keep all the credit for this.'

'That is good of you, I will allow. Is there anything else I need to know about what has been going on?'

'The man who was behind all this, what you might call the brains of the outfit, is lying dead in a farmhouse up on the St Louis road.'

Bridges gave directions to the house

and described the body.

'Was that too your handiwork?' asked the sheriff.

'As to that, Phelps here was going to claim the glory for that killing, but if you wish to do so, then it is nothing to me. I want no further part in any of this.'

'You are a strange one, Bridges. You have taken a good deal upon yourself as touching upon this matter and now you say you want to forget it. Do you not wish folk to congratulate you?'

After giving the question some little thought, Bridges answered 'Since I have come to live in this town, I have found myself in one awkward situation after another. I have been lied to, cheated, threatened with hanging, shot at and I don't know what all else. A short while ago, many in this town were treating me like a leper and wanting to see me strung up. Now, those same people would be regarding me as a public benefactor.

'I tell you straight, life in a town of

this sort is not for me. It is too complicated and you never know where you are. I never had a small fraction of this trouble on the trail.'

'When will you be leaving us?'

'Unless you have any objection, this very day. I want only to wish your aunt a goodbye and then I am heading south for the winter.'

Mrs Larssen was rejoiced to see Chris Bridges safe and sound.

'You have been much in my thoughts and prayers since you lit out last night,' she told him. 'I asked the Lord to set a watch upon you and I mind that he has done so. Leastways, you look to be uninjured and in one piece.'

He didn't know how to tell her that he was about to leave, but the widow Larssen had divined Bridges's purpose without his having to speak. 'Will you have a morsel of food with me before you leave? That is, I suppose, your intention?'

'That it is. Not but that I shall not be sorry to bid you farewell. But the truth is, this town living does not suit me. I never know where I am and things go up and down a little too violently for my taste. One day I am a villain, the next a hero. I prefer a quieter and more ordered existence. I am not ready yet for this.'

When they were seated at the table, Mrs Larssen desired him to ask a blessing on the food.

Bridges said, 'Thank you Lord for the food we have this day. And thank you too for leading me to good people like she whose table I am sitting at. Amen.'

As they ate, Mrs Larssen said hesitantly, 'You know, I am not criticizing, but some of the trouble you have had might have been a consequence of working in a saloon. Perhaps if you had chosen another sort of occupation, things might not have tended in the same direction.'

'That at least is true, ma'am,' said Bridges.

'I have been thinking and this is what

I would say. My brother runs a dry goods store in town. How if I could get him to offer you employment and then you could work there and carry on rooming here with me?'

'That is right good of you, ma'am,' said Bridges, moved by the proposal.

'But?' said Mrs Larssen. 'There is a but?'

'Begging your pardon, ma'am, but there is more to it than the difficulties I have had here, such as nearly getting hanged. Last night I rode out of town and slept under the stars. It was the best night I have had since I bid my friends farewell when they went back to Texas. I cannot stay indoors all the time. It suffocates me. I did not know it until now.'

'I see that. You think that even without the problems you have had, you would still feel the same way?'

'That's the fact of the matter, ma'am. I would.'

Before leaving for good, Bridges looked in on the sheriff for the last time.

'Well, you are leaving then?' said Tucker. 'May we look to see you bringing a herd up to the railhead in the future from time to time?'

'I reckon you may,' said Bridges, 'I make no doubt our paths will cross again.'

'Having you live in my town was interesting, Bridges. Interesting, but not an experience that I would like to repeat as a regular treat, if you take my meaning?'

'Why, I feel just the same way myself,' said Bridges. 'So long.'

11

The journey back to Texas was 700-odd miles as the crow flies, but considerably more when a man is following little tracks and trails and is not in any special hurry. It was the very first time that Bridges had ridden that trail by his own self and he aimed to make the most of it. When you have charge of a few thousand head of cattle, you are not apt to do much in the way of sightseeing; it is all you can do to keep the steers moving along in the right direction, never mind about stopping to admire some little tree or listening to a bird sing.

It took Bridges the better part of a month to get back to the spread where he had been working. He had no idea at all if they would even want him back again after he jumped ship so precipitately. Steady older men like him were hard to find, though, and after some obligatory grumbling he was told that there was still a bed in the bunkhouse where he had been before.

The inside of the wooden bunkhouse was home to seven young men, ranging in age between seventeen and twenty-six. Apart from the two rows of beds, there was a stove at one end and a couple of tables. It was evening and so the boys were taking it easy.

At one table, four men were playing poker for matches, while another was writing a letter to his mother, who lived more than 1,000 miles away. He was feeling a little homesick. The other two men were also lying on their beds, chatting in a desultory fashion. The whole scene was illuminated by two smoky and ineffective oil lamps.

When the door opened all of the men looked up. Any interruption to the monotony was welcome. One of the older card players cried, 'Bridges, you old bastard. We thought you was settled in town for good. Never figured to see you back here again.'

'I knew you boys would be getting up to all sorts of mischief without me to set a watch upon you. I am back now, at any rate.'

One of the young men lying on a nearby bed said teasingly, 'We thought you had give up the trail on account of age, Bridges. Word was that you was no longer up to it.'

The words were no sooner out of his mouth than Bridges had caught ahold of him by his ankle and hauled him off the bed. Play-fighting of this sort was common enough in the bunkhouse and there followed a short wrestling match.

After it was finished, one of the other men said, 'Seriously Bridges, what went wrong up at Stockton? Did you not like town life so well?'

It did not look to Bridges like the time to retell the whole, entire story, and so he limited himself to observing, 'There is worse things than being cold and working hard in the open air. I tell you boys now, I would sooner die on the trail than live in a town again.' Then he took his saddle-roll to the bed at the end of the bunkhouse and lay down on the bed. He was back where he belonged.

THE END

We do hope that you have enjoyed reading this large print book.

Did you know that all of our titles are available for purchase?

We publish a wide range of high quality large print books including:
Romances, Mysteries, Classics
General Fiction
Non Fiction and Westerns

Special interest titles available in large print are:
The Little Oxford Dictionary
Music Book, Song Book
Hymn Book, Service Book

Also available from us courtesy of Oxford University Press:
Young Readers' Dictionary
(large print edition)
Young Readers' Thesaurus
(large print edition)

For further information or a free brochure, please contact us at:
Ulverscroft Large Print Books Ltd.,
The Green, Bradgate Road, Anstey,
Leicester, LE7 7FU, England.
Tel: (00 44) 0116 236 4325
Fax: (00 44) 0116 234 0205

Other titles in the
Linford Western Library:

DUEL OF THE OUTLAWS

John Russell Fearn

The inhabitants of Twin Pines, Arizona lead uneventful, happy lives — until the sudden arrival of Black Yankee and his gang. They shoot the sheriff, take over the place, and Twin Pines spirals downwards into an outlaw town, with lawlessness and sudden death the norm. When Thorn Tanworth, son of the sheriff, returns from his travels, to everyone's astonishment he establishes a mutually beneficial partnership with Black Yankee. But then the two men begin fighting each other for control of the town . . .

KID FURY

Michael D. George

The remote settlement of War Smoke lies quiet — until the calm is shattered by a gunshot. Marshal Matt Fallen and his deputy Elmer spring into action to investigate. Then another shot rings out, and cowboy Billy Jackson's horse gallops into town, dragging its owner's corpse in the dust: one boot still caught in its stirrup, and one hand gripping a smoking gun. Meanwhile, the paths of hired killer Waco Walt Dando and gunfighter Kid Fury are set to converge on War Smoke . . .

FIVE SHOTS LEFT

Ben Bridges

When you have only five shots left, you have to make each one count. Like the outlaw whose quest for revenge didn't go quite according to plan. Or the cowboy who ended up using a most unusual weapon to defeat his enemy. Then there was the store-keeper who had to face his worst fear. A down-at-heel sheepherder who was obliged to set past hatreds aside when renegade Comanches went on the warpath. And an elderly couple who struggled to keep the secret that threatened to tear them apart . . .

VENGEANCE TRAIL

Steve Hayes

A vengeance trail brings Waco McAllum to Santa Rosa, hunting his brother's killers: a grudge which can only be settled by blood. He finds valuable allies in Drifter, Latigo Rawlins, and Gabriel Moonlight — three men who are no strangers to trouble. But along the way, he finds himself on another trail: a crooked one that leads straight to a gang of violent cattle-rustlers. In the final showdown, will Waco get his revenge — or a whole lot more besides?

A ROPE FOR IRON EYES

Rory Black

Notorious bounty hunter Iron Eyes corners the deadly Brand brothers in the house with the red lamp above its door. As the outlaws enjoy themselves, Iron Eyes bursts in with guns blazing. But Matt Brand and his siblings are harder to kill than most wanted men: they fight like tigers, and Iron Eyes is lynched before they ride off. Yet even a rope cannot stop Iron Eyes. And he is determined to resume his deadly hunt, regardless of whoever dares stand in his way.